Merry Mister Meddle

Enid Blyton

Merry Mister Meddle

Illustrated by Rene Cloke

Dragon

Published by Granada Publishing Limited
in Dragon Books 1973
Reprinted 1976, 1979

ISBN 0 583 30192 4

First published by Dean & Son, Ltd 1971
Copyright © Darell Waters Ltd 1954

Granada Publishing Limited
Frogmore, St Albans, Herts AL2 2NF
and
3 Upper James Street, London W1R 4BP
1221 Avenue of the Americas, New York, NY 10020, USA
117 York Street, Sydney, NSW 2000, Australia
100 Skyway Avenue, Toronto, Ontario, Canada M9W 3A6
110 Northpark Centre, 2193 Johannesburg, South Africa
CML Centre, Queen & Wyndham, Auckland 1, New Zealand

Printed in Canada

Granada Publishing®

Contents

Chapter		Page
1.	Meddle and the Mice	7
2.	Meddle Does the Washing	13
3.	Meddle's Treacle Pudding	23
4.	Mister Meddle's New Suit	31
5.	Meddle's Good Turns	42
6.	Meddle in a Fog	59
7.	Meddle Tries To Help	66
8.	Mister Meddle in a Fix	80
9.	Meddle and the Biggle-Gobble	91
10.	Meddle Goes Shopping	103
11.	Now, Mister Meddle!	112
12.	A Surprise for Mister Meddle	118
13.	You're a Nuisance, Mister Meddle!	131
14.	Good-bye, Mister Meddle	137

1: *Meddle and the Mice*

'These tiresome mice!' said Meddle's Aunt Jemima, looking into the larder. 'They've been all over the place, look! Nibbling this, that and the other.'

'What about getting a cat, Aunt?' asked Meddle. 'Wouldn't that be a good idea? She'd soon get rid of the mice for you.'

'You know I don't like cats,' said his aunt. 'Now, Meddle, I'm going out to tea, so please behave yourself till I come back again. I'll be back about eight, and we'll have supper then.'

Off she went. Meddle heaved a sigh of relief when she had gone. Aunt Jemima was always finding fault with him. It was nice to be able to sit down and put his feet up on the mantelpiece and read a book and eat as many peppermints as he liked.

As he sat there reading, he heard a scrabbling sound from the larder. Those mice again!

Meddle put down his book and thought.

'What about a mouse-trap?' he said. 'I know where there is one – out in the shed. I'll get it and set it with a bit of bacon and a bit of cheese. I'll catch those mice for Aunt Jemima. Won't she be pleased?'

He went to fetch the trap. As he came out of the

shed with it, the large black cat from next door came up to him and rubbed against his leg.

'Puss, Puss,' said Meddle, and bent to stroke the cat. Then a bright idea came to him.

'Puss, would you like to sit in our larder and catch a few mice?' he asked. The cat purred. She went indoors with Meddle, and sat down by the fire to wash herself.

'I'll just set this trap, Puss,' said Meddle, 'and then you can go into the larder with it. What with you and the trap, the mice will have a very bad time!'

He went to the larder. He took the cheese from the dish and broke a bit off. He put it in the trap.

Then he unwrapped the bacon and cut a bit of fat from it. He put that on the hook too, and then carefully set the trap. He put it down on the floor.

'There!' he said. 'If that doesn't catch a mouse I'll be surprised!'

He forgot to put the lid back on the cheese-dish. He forgot to wrap the bacon up again. Meddle could never think of little things like that!

He called to the cat. 'Here, Puss! Come and watch for mice here. Come along.'

The cat didn't come. So Meddle went and fetched her and put her firmly down in the larder. Then he shut the door.

It was cold in the larder. The cat didn't like it. She didn't care about mice either, for she was well-fed and never bothered herself to catch them. She mewed and scratched at the door.

'You catch a few mice, and I'll let you out!' said Meddle, and put his feet up on the mantelpiece again. The cat seemed to settle down and there was no sound of either mouse or cat from the larder.

Meddle made himself some tea after a bit and got the biscuit-tin. He wasn't going to bother to cut himself bread-and-butter! He finished all the biscuits in the tin. Then he washed up his tea-things, and went back to read again. But he fell fast asleep, and only woke up when he heard his Aunt Jemima coming in.

'Oh, dear, dear!' she said. 'I missed the bus, and it's half-past eight and I'm so hungry. Why,

Meddle, you haven't even set the supper! Lay the cloth, quickly.'

She stood before the mirror to take off her hat. Suddenly there came a loud noise from the larder.

'CRASH!'

'Whatever's that?' cried Aunt Jemima.

'Oh – I set a mouse-trap there for you,' said Meddle. 'I expect that's the trap catching a mouse!'

'What – a crash like that!' cried his aunt. 'Oh, my goodness – there's another crash – and look, there's milk flowing out under the door! Mice indeed!'

She ran to the larder door and opened it. Out

shot the big black cat, jumped out of the window and disappeared. Aunt Jemima stared in horror at the larder.

'How did that cat get in here? Oh, my goodness, it's eaten the meat-pie I left for supper – and the fish for breakfast – and it's gobbled up the custard I put ready – and it's upset the milk – and look at all this chewed bacon and nibbled cheese! How DID that cat get in here?'

Then she gave a scream. The mouse-trap had gone off and nipped her toe. 'What's that? Oh, the mouse-trap. Meddle, did you put that cheese and bacon in it?'

'Yes, Aunt,' said Meddle in a small voice.

'Well, why didn't you cover up the cheese-dish and wrap up the bacon?' asked his aunt. 'Didn't you know that even if the cat wasn't there to nibble them, the mice would climb up to the shelves and eat them? They wouldn't bother about the trap, if they could see cheese and bacon up here in plenty!'

'No, Aunt,' said Meddle, edging towards the kitchen door.

'Meddle, how did that cat get in here? Did *you* put it in?' said Aunt Jemima, suddenly. 'The larder window's closed. It couldn't possibly have got in by itself.'

'Well, Aunt Jemima – you see, Aunt – it's like this – after all, a cat does catch mice,' began Meddle. 'And I thought ...'

'You thought it would be a very good idea to put that cat into my larder for hours, till it began to get really hungry and eat all our supper!' cried his aunt. 'Come here, Meddle, come here!'

But Meddle was gone! 'Good thing too!' said his aunt. 'There's only supper enough for one – an egg and bread-and-butter. Just wait till you come in, Meddle, just wait!'

Poor Meddle. He does his best, but it's such a bad best, isn't it?

2: *Meddle Does the Washing*

Meddle was staying with his Aunt Jemima. He didn't like Mondays because it was his aunt's washing-day then, and she groaned and grumbled all day long.

'Oh, how dirty you make your shirts, Meddle! Anyone would think you lived in a chimney, they're so black! And look at these hankies of yours! Have you used them to wipe up spilt ink or something?'

'Oh, dear – it's washing day again!' Meddle would think. 'I must really get out of Aunt's way. She grumbles all day long – goodness knows why! There doesn't seem to be anything much in washing. You just get hot water, make a fine lather of soap and get on with it. I'm sure I could do it easily enough without any grumbling!'

He watched his aunt making the lather in the wash-tub. He liked all the bubbly, frothy lather. He dipped his fingers into it. It felt soft and silky.

'The better lather you have, the easier it is to wash the clothes,' said his aunt. 'But it's difficult to get a good, frothy lather these days. Get out of the way, Meddle. You'll have the tub over in a minute.'

Now the next Monday Meddle's aunt had a pain in her back. She sat in her armchair and groaned:

'Oh, dear, oh, dear! I can't do the washing today. I've such a pain in my back. I must do it tomorrow.'

Meddle looked at his aunt in alarm. 'Tomorrow! Oh, no, Aunt. You promised to take me to the fair.'

'Well, washing is more important than going to the fair,' said his aunt.

Meddle didn't think it was at all. He went into the scullery and looked at the pile of washing there. Horrid washing! Now he wouldn't be able to go to the fair!

Then an idea came into his mind. Why shouldn't *he* do the washing? It always looked very easy. And if he got a really fine lather it would be easier still.

'I'll go to Dame Know-all and ask her for a little growing-spell,' thought Meddle. 'I'll pop it into the wash-tub with the lather, and it will grow marvellously so that I can do all the washing in no time at all.'

He went off to Dame Know-all. She was out. Meddle looked round her little shop. Ah – there on a shelf was a bottle marked 'Growing-spells.' Just what he wanted!

He put six pence down on the counter, took down the bottle, unscrewed the lid and emptied a small growing-spell into his hand. It was like a tiny blue pea.

He put back the bottle and went out of the shop.

He ran back to his aunt's in glee. Aha! It took a clever fellow like him to think how to make washing easy! What a fine soapy lather he could get. How all the dirt would roll out of the clothes when he popped them into the lather and squeezed them!

He peeped in at his aunt. She was still in her chair. She had fallen asleep. Meddle softly closed the door and went into the scullery.

He filled the wash-tub with boiling hot water and popped in the soap flakes his aunt used. He swished them about with his hand, and a bubbly lather began to rise up in the tub.

Then Meddle put in the little blue growing-spell. It dissolved in the water and made it bluer than before. A little blue steam came up and mixed with the soapy lather.

And the lather began to grow!

Hundreds and hundreds of soapy bubbles began to form in the tub, and frothed out over the side, shining with all the colours of the rainbow.

'Good!' said Meddle, pleased, and he stuffed all the dirty clothes into the frothing lather. He pushed them down into the hot water, and began to squeeze them. But he couldn't do that for long, because the lather had grown so much that it frothed right up to his face. Bubbles burst and his eyes began to smart. He blew the lather away from his cheeks.

But it went on growing! He had taken a far too powerful growing-spell from the bottle, and thou-

sands and thousands of soapy bubbles were frothing up.

The lather fell out of the tub and went on
growing. Soon Meddle was waist-deep in bubbles!
He kicked at them.

'Stop growing! That's enough! How can I possibly do the washing when I can't get near the tub?
Stop, I tell you!'

But the lather didn't stop. It crept along the
floor, frothing out beautifully. It grew higher. It
sent bubbles all over the top of the table, and on to
the gas-stove. Gracious, what a sight!

Meddle began to feel alarmed. 'STOP!' he
shouted. 'Are you deaf? STOP!'

But bubbles went on growing by the hundred
and frothed about everywhere. Some of them
rolled out of the window. The bubbly lather-
stream went through the door into the kitchen. It
frothed over the floor there, looking very peculiar
indeed. Meddle began to get really frightened. He
made his way out of the scullery, where the bubbles
were now up to his neck, and found a broom. He
attacked the lather with all his might, trying to
sweep it back into the scullery, so that he could
close the door on it.

But the more he swept, the quicker it grew! It
was dreadful. Thank goodness the door into the
parlour was shut. Whatever would his aunt think
if she saw a mass of froth creeping into the parlour?

The larder door was open, and the lather went
there, frothing all over the shelves. Oh, dear! It

soon hid the meat-pie and the cold pudding that Aunt Jemima had planned for dinner that day.

Aunt Jemima slept peacefully in the parlour. She had had a bad night and was glad to rest a little, with a cushion at her back. But when the noise of Meddle sweeping hard in the kitchen came to her ears, she awoke and sat up.

'What's that? What can Meddle be doing? The kitchen doesn't want sweeping!' she said to herself. She looked at the shut door and wondered if she should call out to Meddle to stop.

And then she saw something very peculiar indeed. A little line of lather was creeping under the

18

door! A little drip of lather was coming through the key-hole! Aunt Jemima started as if she couldn't believe her eyes. What was this strange thing creeping under the door? And whatever was coming through the key-hole? She wondered if she was still asleep and dreaming.

'Meddle,' she called, 'what are you doing? Open the door. There's something queer happening.'

Meddle heard what his aunt said – but he certainly wasn't going to open the door and let all the bubbles into the parlour! It was quite bad enough already in the kitchen. The froth was almost up to his shoulders. He couldn't even *see* his legs! Sometimes the bubbles went up his nose and made him sneeze and choke. His eyes smarted. He felt very upset.

Aunt Jemima watched the line of bubbles creeping under the door in alarm. As soon as the lather was properly in the parlour it began to grow very quickly. It frothed up into the air, and Aunt Jemima got out of her chair in fright. What was all this?

She trod through the bubbles and opened the door into the kitchen. That was a terrible mistake! At once a great cloud of soapy bubbles swept over her, and she was almost smothered in them. She screamed.

'Meddle, what *is* this? What's happening? Good gracious, I can hardly see the top of your head!'

'Oh, Aunt, oh, Aunt, it's all because of a growing-spell I put into the wash-tub to make a fine

lather,' wept Meddle. 'It won't stop growing now.
Oh, what are we to do?'

'Well! Of all the donkeys, you're the biggest,
Meddle!' shouted his aunt, trying to make her way

through the bubbles. 'Open the garden door!
Sweep the lather into the garden. Don't let it fill
the house!'

Meddle groped his way to the door, coughing
and sneezing. He opened it. A great wave of froth
immediately rolled out. More and more followed.
It went down the garden path, and all the passers-
by stood still in astonishment to see such a sight.

They had to get out of the way of the lather

when it got to the hedge. It frothed over it and made its way down the road. Aunt Jemima watched it.

'Won't it ever stop?' said Meddle, really scared.

'It will stop when the growing-spell is worn out,' said his aunt, in a very grim voice.

The spell didn't wear itself out for four hours. By that time the lather had reached the village, and

all the children were paddling about in the bubbles, having a lovely time. How they laughed and shouted!

But at last the froth grew smaller and smaller. The bubbles burst and disappeared and no more grew. By one o'clock there was not a single bubble left. The wonderful lather had gone.

Meddle was terribly hungry by this time. So was his aunt. She went to the larder and looked at the soapy meat-pie and the cold pudding. Then she went out to the henhouse and found two new-laid eggs. She brought them back and put them in a saucepan on the stove to boil.

'You can have the pie and the pudding,' she said to Meddle. But when he tried to eat them, he made a terrible face.

'Oooh! They taste of soap! Can I have an egg, Aunt?'

'There are only two, and I'm having them both,' said his aunt. 'Eat up the pie and the pudding.'

So poor Meddle had to, and they tasted far worse than any medicine he had ever had in his life.

'I shall have to do the washing tomorrow, just as I planned,' said his aunt. 'Next time you want to meddle in anything, Meddle, tell me before you start. It would save such a lot of trouble! As for the fair, don't dare to mention it! It might make me put you into the wash-tub with the dirty washing!'

3: *Meddle's Treacle Pudding*

One day Meddle went to take his aunt some daffodils out of his garden. She wasn't feeling very pleased with him, and he thought it would be a good idea to make her a little present of flowers.

She was delighted. 'Well, there now, Meddle, if that isn't kind of you!' she said. 'You're a silly, meddlesome fellow most of the time, but not always. Stay and have dinner with me.'

'What are you having for dinner?' asked Meddle.

'Cold meat, baked potatoes and a nice jam sponge pudding,' said his aunt.

'Couldn't you make it a treacle pudding instead?' begged Meddle. 'I do so like treacle puddings.'

'I would, if I'd got any treacle,' said Aunt Jemima. 'But I haven't. Not a drop! So you'll have to make do with a jam sponge pudding if you are going to stay and have dinner with me, Meddle.'

'All right,' said Meddle, and he picked up the morning paper to read whilst his aunt bustled round to do her work. But she didn't like that.

'Now, Meddle, don't you laze about,' she said. 'If you're going to spend the morning with me, you'll have to do something. I can't bear people who laze about.'

'Oh, dear,' said Meddle. 'Well, what do you want me to do?'

'I've got the workmen doing odd jobs in my scullery today,' said Aunt Jemima. 'You go and see if you can help them. Hammer in some nails, or something.'

Meddle wandered off into the scullery, but after he had hammered somebody's fingers, and upset all the tools into the wet sink, the workmen didn't want him any more. Nobody ever wanted Meddle for long!

One of them gave him a little pot with something yellow-brown at the bottom of it.

'Go and put this on the kitchen stove and stir it

every now and again,' he said. 'That will keep you
out of mischief.'

Meddle took the little pot. He put it on the hot
kitchen stove. Then he looked round for something to stir with. He found an old spoon.

By the time he got back to the stove the yellow-
brown stuff in the little pot was bubbling nicely.
Meddle peered at it.

'My goodness me, if it isn't treacle!' he said.
'Look at that now! A pot full of melting treacle,
and Aunt Jemima hasn't any at all.'

He stirred it. It wasn't treacle, of course, it was
glue. But that didn't enter Meddle's head at all. He
was sure it was good rich treacle. He stirred it well.

'This would taste lovely on our pudding,' he thought. 'It's just what we want. I wonder if the workmen would mind if I had two big spoonfuls for our pudding. I'll ask them.'

So he popped his head into the scullery and called to them. 'I say, can I have some of this stuff on my pudding, men?'

The workmen thought he was trying to be funny. They laughed. 'Take what you like for your

pudding!' called one. 'It's not what *we'd* choose – but if you like it, take it!'

Meddle was delighted. He went to tell his Aunt, but she had gone out shopping. She had left the pudding steaming on the stove. Meddle began to feel hungry. How lovely to have a nice sponge pudding with treacle all over it. Oooooh!

He laid the table. He got the dish ready for the pudding. He took the baked potatoes out of the oven, and wrapped them up in a napkin and put them into a dish to keep hot.

Aunt Jemima was pleased to see all he had done when she got home. She beamed at Meddle. 'Well, well – you *can* be useful when you try. I'm pleased with you, Meddle. You shall have two helpings of the pudding.'

Meddle didn't say anything about the treacle. He thought he would give his aunt a nice surprise. He left it simmering on the stove.

Soon Meddle and his aunt were sitting down to have their dinner. They ate their cold meat, potatoes and pickles, and then Aunt Jemima went to get the pudding. Soon it was on its hot dish, and Aunt Jemima carried it to the table. 'Now bless us all, if I haven't forgotten to warm up the jam for the pudding!' she said.

'It's all right,' said Meddle. 'I've got some hot treacle for it! Sit down, Aunt, and I'll get it. It will be *such* a treat!'

He went to get it. He poured some of it out of the glue-pot into a sauceboat, and took it to the table. 'All thick and hot!' he said, and his mouth watered as he thought of the treat in store. He poured half of it over his aunt's pudding. He poured the rest over his own helping.

'It looks a bit peculiar,' said Aunt Jemima, doubtfully. 'And it smells funny, too.'

'It'll *taste* all right!' said Meddle. 'Try it, Aunt Jemima!'

They both took a big spoonful of their pudding, and then made two dreadful faces. Their teeth stuck together. They couldn't chew, they couldn't speak, they couldn't swallow!

Aunt Jemima stumbled to the bathroom to get some water. Meddle's eyes nearly fell out of his head with horror. 'It's glue!' he thought. 'It's glue! Oh, why did I meddle with it? Horrible, horrible, horrible!'

He couldn't say a word, and neither could his aunt, even after she had drunk glass after glass of water. But she *did* a lot. She chased him round the room sixteen times and smacked him hard. Then she chased him out of the house and up the road. Meddle raced away, large tears running down his sticky cheeks.

'Now, then, what's the matter?' said Mr. Plod the policeman, meeting Meddle suddenly round a corner. 'What are you in such a hurry for? Just you stop and explain.'

But all that poor Meddle could say was 'Oooof-ooof-ooof!' so he had to go with Mr. Plod, who thought he was being rude. And I'm very much afraid he'll have to stay at the police-station till the glue is worn off!

4: *Mister Meddle's New Suit*

'Oh, dear — I really do need a new suit!' said
Mister Meddle one summer morning, as he looked
at himself in the glass. 'My trousers are torn, my
coat is dirty, and really I am surprised that my
shirt holds together. As for my stockings, they are
nothing but holes!'

He went to look in his purse. There was five
pence there, and that was all.

'Can't buy even a pair of socks with that,' said
Mister Meddle. 'I've got to go to tea with Aunt
Jemima this afternoon, too. Well, she'll just have
to put up with my old clothes!'

He set off to go to tea with his aunt at about
three o'clock. He had washed his hands and
brushed his hair but he hadn't mended his trousers
or darned the holes in his stockings. That was
much too much trouble.

It was a very windy day indeed. Mister Meddle
wished he had a kite to fly. The boys and girls had
all got out their kites and were having fun with
them. The big windmill on the common was whiz-
zing round and round. Mister Meddle's hat blew
off three times, and he got cross.

He picked it up out of the dust and looked at it.
'Now *you've* got dirty, too!' he said. He brushed it

hard with his hand and slapped it against himself. 'I do wish I had some nice clothes. I'm tired of looking like a tramp!'

He climbed over a stile to go across a field. He saw something peculiar flapping along the ground towards him and stared in astonishment.

'What is it? Good gracious! It's a shirt. A blue silk shirt! Now, whatever is it doing dancing about in this field all alone?'

He picked it up. It was exactly his size. 'This is a very strange thing,' said Meddle, and looked all round to see if by chance anyone had dropped the shirt. But there was no one about at all.

Then he saw something else coming towards him. How queer! This time it was a pair of trousers! They were a bright red, and had stripes of blue running down the sides. Very, very unusual, thought Mister Meddle.

He picked up the trousers and tried them against himself. They seemed just his size. He felt very excited indeed.

'I do believe – yes, I do believe that my wish has come true!' he said to himself. 'I was saying how I wished I had some new clothes – and now here are some dancing across the field to me!'

Then he saw something else – something brightly red, like the trousers, with little blue buttons in front. A coat! A really beautiful coat!. Meddle could hardly believe his eyes.

'What a bit of luck! Here's a coat too. Yes, there's no doubt my wish has come true. And my

goodness me, here come a pair of blue socks! I'll look about for some shoes, too – and a new hat would be nice.'

But he couldn't find either shoes or hat. Still, never mind – he had a wonderful set of new clothes, and he meant to put them on at once. So he went into a tumbledown cowshed nearby, took off his old clothes, and put on the new ones – the fine blue shirt, the red coat and trousers, and the blue socks. Lovely!

'I wish I could see myself,' thought Meddle. 'I must look awfully grand. What shall I do with my horrid old clothes? Here, goat, you can have them!'

A billy-goat had just put his head in at the shed door. Meddle threw him the clothes. The goat looked surprised. It sniffed at them, and then began to chew them up. It didn't mind what it ate. Meddle's old clothes would make a very good meal indeed!

Meddle went joyfully out of the shed, dressed in blue and red. Whatever would Aunt Jemima say? She would hardy know him!

His aunt stared at him in surprise when she opened the door for him. 'Meddle! You've been spending far too much money on new clothes! You bad boy.'

'I haven't spent a penny,' said Meddle. 'Aunt, I wished for some new clothes, and they all came dancing up to me!'

'I don't believe a word of it!' said his aunt at once. Meddle looked very hurt.

'I'm telling the truth,' he said. 'They came dancing over the field right to my feet. Don't you think I look nice, Aunt? You're always saying I ought to have new clothes.'

'You look smarter than I've ever seen you,' said Aunt Jemima. 'Come along in to tea. There are some new ginger buns, and some lovely honey from my neighbour's bees. I hope you won't spill it down your new suit!'

Now, in the middle of tea, when Meddle was spreading new honey on his bread, there came a knock at the door. Aunt Jemima went to open it. Meddle heard someone talking to his aunt in a very worried voice. It was Mrs. Buzz, the bee-woman from next door.

'Whatever's the matter with her?' said Meddle to himself. 'Well, all I hope is that she keeps Aunt talking for a long time, then I can have lots more honey.'

He listened again – and then his hair stood up on his head in horror.

'My dear, I pegged them all out on my line, and when I went to take them in, they'd gone!' said Mrs. Buzz's voice. 'Quite gone – the blue shirt, the red trousers and coat, and even the blue socks. What Mr. Buzz will say I really *don't* know. I suppose the strong wind blew them away.'

Meddle dropped a blob of honey on his coat; he got such a shock to hear all this that his hand trembled like a jelly. Oh, dear, oh dear – so that's where his new clothes had come from – Mrs. Buzz's clothes-line! Why hadn't he thought of that?

His Aunt Jemima came into the room, looking very stern indeed. Mrs. Buzz was behind her. She gave a scream when she saw Meddle.

'Oh! He's got all the lost clothes on! Oh, the rascal!'

'Meddle! How dare you take clothes off somebody's clothes-line?' said his aunt, in such a terrible voice that Meddle shook and shivered.

'I didn't. They danced over the field to me,' said poor Meddle, in a shaky voice.

'Take them off. Put on your old clothes and give these back to Mrs. Buzz,' commanded his aunt.

'I c-c-can't,' said Meddle. 'I gave my old clothes to the billy-g-g-goat to eat!'

'You're a wicked fellow!' said Mrs. Buzz. 'I'm off to get the policeman!'

She ran out of the room, and poor Meddle was terribly frightened. He jumped out of the window, and began to run home as fast as he could.

Just as he was getting over the stile, he saw a man coming towards him. As soon as he saw him, this man gave a loud shout, and rushed at the surprised Mister Meddle. He gave him such a blow that Meddle fell back over the stile again.

'You've got my clothes on!' shouted the man. It was Mr. Buzz! 'How dare you! You give them to me at once!'

Meddle got up and raced away. Mr. Buzz looked so fierce that he was afraid of him. Meddle rushed to the cowshed and disappeared inside. The goat was still there, chewing what looked like a heap of rags.

'Shoo, goat, shoo!' cried Meddle. The goat looked surprised, and backed away with a bit of Meddle's shirt hanging from its mouth. Meddle groaned.

'Is that all that's left of my shirt? And, oh dear, look at this coat – both sleeves have been eaten – and there's no sign of my socks – and you've eaten one leg of my trousers right up to the knee.'

The goat then heard Mr. Buzz coming and moved to the door. It felt cross. Was someone else coming to disturb it at its meal? When Mr. Buzz

peered round the door the goat ran at him and butted him hard. He rolled over and over on the grass outside.

Meddle hurriedly took off his new clothes and put on his poor sleeveless coat and his half-eaten trousers. He couldn't put on a shirt or socks because they had been eaten. Then he went cautiously to the door.

The goat was having a fine game with poor Mr. Buzz! It was dancing all round him, butting him whenever he tried to get up. Mr. Buzz was getting angrier and angrier.

Meddle shouted to Mr. Buzz: 'Look, here are

your clothes! You can get them when the goat lets you!' He threw down the clothes and then raced off home, looking more like a tramp than ever, in his half-chewed, ragged coat and trousers.

He looked at himself in the glass when he got home. 'I can't go out like this! I'll have to put on an overall and go to work somewhere, to earn money for new things. Just as I'm feeling lazy, too!'

He wondered if Mr. and Mrs. Buzz would come along with the policeman, and whether his aunt

would come to spank him. Meddle thought it very likely indeed.

He found his overall, put it on, packed a little bag, and then went to catch a bus to the next town. He locked his door and put the key in his pocket.

'I'll get a job miles away!' he said, 'even if it means working hard and wearing an overall for weeks till I can buy a new suit.'

So, when Aunt Jemima came along to spank him she couldn't find him, and when Mr. and Mrs. Buzz came with a policeman he wasn't there.

Poor Meddle! He won't believe in wishes coming true again, will he?

5: *Meddle's Good Turns*

Aunt Jemima was very cross with Meddle. He had been staying with her for a few days, and had managed to upset everybody, even the cat.

He had made the cook cross because he had gone into her larder at night and eaten all the jam tarts she had made for the next day's dinner. He had upset the gardener by borrowing his best spade and leaving it somewhere where it couldn't be found.

And he had upset the cat by treading three times on its tail in one day.

'You are very unkind, Meddle,' said his aunt.

'I'm *not*,' said Meddle. 'It's the cat that's untidy – leaving her tail about all over the place for people to tread on. I believe she does it on purpose.'

Then he upset his aunt by telling her not to bother about watering her plants, he'd do it for her – and he took the wrong jug, and used up all the day's milk to water the plants.

'But couldn't you *see* it was milk when it came pouring out?' said his aunt, exasperated.

'I didn't look,' said Meddle. 'And if I *had* looked and seen it, I should just have thought your water was a funny colour, that's all. I took the jug you told me.'

'No, you didn't,' said his aunt in her very crossest voice. 'Meddle, I feel I'm going to spank you very soon. Very, very soon. I can feel my hands beginning to tingle. I can . . .'

Meddle backed away in alarm. 'I'm sorry, Aunt Jemima. Really I am. I'm going out now so I shan't worry you any more this morning.'

'Well, Meddle, you'd better turn over a new leaf and try to help people instead of hindering them,' said his aunt. 'You go out, and when you come back you just tell me all the *good* things you've done. If you've any to tell I might not feel so spankable towards you.'

Meddle put on his hat and went out in a hurry, treading on the cat's tail once more. The cat spat and dug its claws into his leg. Meddle howled, leapt into the air, and fell down the steps.

His aunt slammed the door and comforted the cat. The cook put her head into the hall.

'Has he gone?' she said. 'Ha, that's a pity, I've just discovered that a meat-pie is missing, and I've got a rolling pin here to punish the thief.'

'He's gone,' said Aunt Jemima. 'He's going to turn over a new leaf, and do some good deeds for a change.'

'I'll believe that when I hear he's done some,' said the cook, and disappeared with the cat close behind her.

Meddle wandered down the street, a big hole in

his stocking where the cat had scratched him. He looked very solemn. He really and truly *would* do a good deed – if he could find one to do. There were always so many to do when he didn't want

to – but now that he wanted to, it was difficult to find one.

He saw an old lady crossing the road with a basket full of goods. He ran to her at once, and tried to take away her basket, meaning to carry it for her.

She screamed at the top of her voice. 'Help! Help! He's robbing me! Help!'

Then up ran two men and Mr. Plod, the policeman. 'What are you doing to this old lady?' de-

manded Mr. Plod. 'Oh, it's you, Meddle, is it? What sort of silly trick are you up to now?'

'I was about to do a good turn,' said Meddle haughtily. 'Can't I carry an old lady's basket for her if I want to?'

And he went off, feeling very angry, his nose in the air. He was most annoyed. All that fuss, and he had only wanted to carry a basket for somebody!

He walked down a long street. A woman came out of a gate with a dustbin and dumped it down by her gate, almost on Meddle's toe. He jumped and glared.

'Sorry,' said the woman. 'It's dustbin day. We all have to put our dustbins out for the dustman to empty.'

'Dear, dear!' said Meddle. 'Do you mean to say you have to drag out those heavy dustbins all by yourself? That *is* a shame!'

'Oh, I don't mind for myself, I'm strong,' said the woman. 'But I'm sorry for old Mrs. Lacy, who lives down the road there. Poor old thing, she finds it a heavy job.'

The woman went indoors and Meddle went on down the street. He thought he would offer to take out Mrs. Lacy's dustbins for her. That would really be a good turn to do.

There was only one house that had no dustbins outside. That must be Mrs. Lacy's, thought Meddle. Poor old thing – she hadn't been able to carry them out herself, and nobody else had offered to

do so for her. Well, he, Meddle, would do everything necessary!

He went in at the back way and had a look
round. My, my, there were three big dustbins there
– no wonder the poor old thing couldn't lift them.
Meddle knocked at the back door to tell Mrs. Lacy
he was going to take her heavy dustbins out for
her.

'Blim, blam!' he knocked, and waited. But nobody came to the door. 'Must be deaf,' thought
Meddle, and knocked again. 'Old ladies often are,
poor things.'

But even his much louder knocking didn't bring
Mrs. Lacy to the door. Meddle looked at the dust-

bins. He could quite well take them out into the roadway now, and tell Mrs. Lacy when she at last came to the door. Or maybe she was out and he could tell her when she came back.

So, with much puffing and panting, Meddle got one of the dustbins on to his back and staggered with it to the road. He set it down with a bang. Gracious, it was heavy!

Back he went for the second one, which was even heavier, and dumped that beside the first one. He mopped his forehead and panted. This really was a good deed! He felt quite exhausted already.

'Only one more,' thought Meddle and went back for it. He soon had that one beside the ohers, and then he saw that he was only just in time, because the dustcart was coming down the street already.

'Ha! Just at the right moment,' said Mister Meddle, pleased. 'I'll wait here till the dustmen have emptied the three bins belonging to Mrs. Lacy, and then I'll take them all back again. She *will* be so pleased! If it hadn't been for me coming along just at this moment, she wouldn't have had them stood outside, or emptied, or taken back to their place!'

He waited till the dustmen came along. They lifted the first bin up and emptied it into the cart. A terrific cloud of dust went up and everyone sneezed.

Then the second one was emptied, and then the third. Meddle trotted back with the empty dustbins, feeling very good and virtuous. He wished his Aunt Jemima could see him now. She would be sorry she had thought so unkindly of him.

He stood the dustbins in their places and knocked at the back door again. The next-door-neighbour heard him and popped her head over the fence.

'No good knocking. They're out,' she said.

'Oh, well, never mind,' said Meddle, giving the woman a sweet smile, much to her surprise. 'I only wanted to say I'd taken out the full dustbins, and brought them back again when they were emptied. Good day!'

And with another sweet smile Meddle went up the path to the front, and was gone. He ambled down the road feeling very pleased with himself. He thought he wouldn't mind doing *another* good turn. But what? He came to a gateway. Beside it stood a pot of white paint, and a brush stood in the pot. Nobody was about.

'The man must have gone in to his dinner,' thought Meddle looking at the gate. 'What was he doing? Oh – repainting the name of the house. Dear me, it's so faint I can hardly read it.'

He bent to see what it was. It really was very faint indeed, and looked almost as if the painter had tried to take away the name before repainting it. Perhaps he wanted to do it differently this time, with bigger letters, thought Meddle.

'Fir-Trees,' he read at last. He laughed. 'Well, well – isn't that just like some people! They call a

house Fir-Trees, and the only trees in the garden are rose bushes!'

He looked at the pot of paint. Wouldn't it be a very good turn if he painted the name again on the gate? The owner would be so pleased to come out from his dinner and find someone had done his work for him.

'I'm sure I could paint nicely,' thought Meddle picking up the paint-brush and looking at the white paint dripping off it on to the pavement below. 'It would be a nice job to do. Just the kind I like. Pity I haven't an overall or something, but I'll be careful not to mess my clothes.'

He began. He could just see the name 'Fir-Trees'

well enough to follow the letters over again with the white paint. He went over the line here and there, but he didn't notice that. He also dropped most of the paint on to the pavement and some on his coat and a good deal on his shoes, but he didn't notice that either.

'I'm doing another good deed,' said Meddle to himself. 'Really, Aunt Jemima has no right to scold me as she does. I can do more good deeds than she does. *She* would never have thought of taking out those dustbins, or of painting the name on this gate.'

Now, up the road, in the garden of the house whose dustbins Meddle had carried out to be emptied, quite a disturbance was going on. There was a lot of shouting and banging of dustbin lids, and the next-door-neighbour popped her head over the fence to see whatever the matter was.

'Matter! Matter enough!' shouted a big, round, red-faced fellow with enormous black eyebrows. 'Someones stolen the hen and pig food out of my bins! Look here – this is where the hen feed was – and it's empty.' Bang! Down went a dustbin lid and another came up. 'And here's where the corn was and it's empty!' Bang! Down went that dustbin lid. 'And here's where the pig-food was, and it's empty!' Bang!

'Don't glare at me like that,' said the woman. '*I* haven't taken them. They've all been emptied into the dustman's cart,'

The red-faced man's eyebrows shot up till they

almost disappeared. '*What!* Into the *dust-cart!* Say that again, Mrs. Brown.'

She said it again, and then moved a little farther away, afraid that her neighbour was going to burst with fury and rage.

'Who did that?' he spluttered at last. 'The dustmen? Did they dare to come and collect my dustbins? Why, they know I always burn my own rubbish and never want anything emptied!'

'No. It wasn't the dustmen,' said Mrs. Brown. 'It was a funny-looking fellow with a long nose and untidy hair. He was banging at your back door to tell you he had taken out your bins to be emptied.'

The red-faced man could hardly believe this extraordinary tale. 'Where is this fellow?' he said at last.

'He went away,' said Mrs. Brown. 'You might find him about the district if you go and look, though. You can't mistake his long nose – a real meddling nose it is, always being poked into somebody else's business, I should think.'

'It won't be poked into *mine* again,' said the red-faced man grimly, and he gritted his teeth together with a very nasty noise as he went to his front gate.

He walked down the road. Then he saw Meddle, who was still very busy painting the name on the gate. He had done as far as Fir-Tre . .' and only had the letters e and s to do.

The red-faced man took a look at Meddle's long and pointed nose. Ha, there was no mistaking that! He tiptoed up behind him meaning to pounce on him unawares, but Meddle heard him gritting his teeth and looked round suddenly.

'GAAAAAAH!' yelled the man and flung himself on Meddle, who promptly sat down in the paint-pot and couldn't get out.

The brush flew up into the air and hit the red-faced man over one eye. He stopped in surprise – and at that very moment out came the man who had been meaning to paint his gate and had gone in to his dinner.

He was very surprised to see one man sitting in his paint-pot and another man wiping white paint out of his eye.

'What's all this?' he cried angrily. 'Hey, get up out of my paint-pot, you! What are you doing here?'

'Sir,' said Meddle haughtily, trying to get up, but not being able to, 'sir, I was doing you a good turn. I was painting the name on your gate for you.'

The man looked at his gate and gave a howl of rage. 'What have you done that for? Fir-Trees! You've gone and put Fir-Trees!'

'Except for the last e and s I have,' said Meddle. 'That's what the name was, wasn't it? Though I must tell you I think it's a silly name because there are only rose bushes in your garden.'

'Well, what do you suppose I rubbed the name out for?' shouted the man. 'I was going to put up 'Rose-Cot' but I had to go in for my dinner. Now you've gone and put 'Fir-Trees' again. How dare you meddle? How dare you interfere? You come

along in and I'll douse your head in cold water. I'll...'

'No. *I* want him,' said the red-faced man, and put his heavy hand on poor Meddle's shoulder. 'Do you

know what he's done? He's gone and let the dust-men empty all my bins of hen-food and corn and pig-food into their cart! Grrrrrrrrr!'

He growled like a dog and shook Meddle so hard that he came off the paint-pot, and rolled into the road. Both men pounced on him at once, but the red-faced man put his foot into the paint-pot and fell over. The other man fell on top of him, and Meddle scrambled up quickly to rush away.

How he ran! He puffed and he panted, and ran till he felt he would burst. He sank down on a seat at a bus stop and buried his face in his hanky.

'Oh, dear! Two good turns gone west! How was I to know the silly fellow kept his hen-food in his dustbins? I thought old Mrs. Lacy lived there. And how am I to know if people suddenly change their silly minds about the names of their silly houses? Rose-Cot! Ooooh, what a name!'

Now, who should come by to catch the next bus just then but his Aunt Jemima. Meddle saw her and moved up to give her room. He forgot that he had been sitting in a pot of white paint, and he had covered the seat with white patches. Before she could stop herself Aunt Jemima had sat down on a patch of wet paint. She leapt up again with a cry and craned her head over her back.

'Oh! My best black velvet skirt! You did that on purpose, Meddle! You wicked fellow! Now you just come along home with me, and I'll show you what happens to people who put white paint on seats for me to sit on. A good spanking is what you need!'

But he didn't get it, because he was all over white paint! Poor Meddle – if only he didn't meddle in other people's affairs he would get on much better, wouldn't he?

6: *Meddle in a Fog*

'I'm going out to buy some sweets, Aunt Jemima,' said Meddle. 'Do you want any letters posted?'

'No, I don't. And you're not going out in this fog, Meddle,' said his aunt, firmly.

'What fog? Dear me, I hadn't noticed that it was foggy,' said Meddle, looking out of the window in surprise.

'No. You never notice things like that, unless it's pointed out to you,' said his aunt. 'The times you go out in the rain without your umbrella! The times you . . .'

Meddle scowled. If Aunt Jemima was going to scold him all afternoon he didn't want to stay in! Anyway, the fog wasn't very thick. It wouldn't in the least matter going out in it.

He got up. 'The fog's not too thick,' he said. 'I think I'll just go out and get my sweets, Aunt Jemima.'

'No. Sit down,' said his aunt. 'You know that old Mrs. Trottle may be coming to tea this afternoon if it isn't *too foggy* – and I want you to change into your clean suit, and wash your dirty hands and brush your hair. Otherwise you certainly can't come and have tea with us – and that means you won't have any cake or jam sandwich.'

'Oooh – is there to be a special tea?' said Meddle, who was greedy. 'All right, I'll go and change now, and get as clean as I can.'

But he didn't go upstairs to change. He tip-toed to the back door and let himself out! 'I'm going to get my sweets, whatever horrid old Aunt Jemima says!' he thought. '*I* shan't get lost in the fog! Aunt will never know, because she will think I am up-stairs changing my clothes and washing myself!'

And out into the fog he went. It wasn't too bad, really. He could see about three yards in front of him, and he made his way to the sweet-shop quite easily. He bought his sweets and then went to look round the pet-shop next door. It was a good thing he had no more money to spend or he would have bought a black dog, a white cat, two mice and a parrot that would say 'Pass the salt, please,' and then cackle loudly just like a hen that has laid an egg. Meddle thought it was wonderful.

When he got out of the pet-shop the fog was much thicker. Oh, dear – he could hardly see his way at all now! He groped down the street, feeling the railings at one side.

He got to the corner and went round it. Then he wondered if it was the wrong corner. He looked at the names on the gates. Oh, dear – he didn't know them at all!

'Cosy-Cot! Why, that's not a house near us,' he said to himself! 'And here's Green Gates – I never remember seeing that in my life! I'd better go back to the corner.'

So he did, and crossed the road there and went over to the other side. 'This must be right now,' he thought. 'Now – down this road, round the corner, turn to the left, and there I shall be, at home! I shall creep in at the back door, go upstairs to wash and change – and Aunt Jemima will never, never know I've been out. Wouldn't I get a spanking if she did!'

But he didn't come to his aunt's house. He stopped in despair. 'I must be lost! This fog's so thick, now, I can hardly see. And it's getting dark, too. Bother! What shall I do?'

He went a little farther on, hoping to meet someone and ask the way. But he didn't meet anyone at all. He stood still and frowned.

Was he anywhere near his home at all? He *must* find it because if he didn't Aunt Jemima would send out a search-party for him, and would be so cross when he was found and brought back. Besides he would miss that lovely tea if he wasn't quick!

He thought of the tea. Chocolate cake with cream in the middle – jam sandwich that melted in his mouth – and perhaps some of those short-bread biscuits that Aunt Jemima made so well. He set off walking again.

But still he couldn't find out where he was. And now it really was getting darker. 'I'll have to go in at a gate, knock on a front door, and ask how to get to my own home,' thought Meddle at last. So he went in at the nearest gate, marched up the path and banged on the front door.

Footsteps came down the hall, which was dark. The door opened and someone peered out.

'Please,' said Meddle, 'I'm lost in the fog. I want to get home quickly because my aunt is having a very nice tea – so could you tell me where I live?'

'Yes,' said the person at the door, and a hand came out and boxed him smartly on the ear. 'You live here!'

And Meddle was dragged indoors and the door was slammed shut. It was his Aunt Jemima speaking to him! He had chosen his very own house to come and ask at for help! Well, well, well – how exactly like poor old Meddle!

'Oh, Aunt Jemima – oh dear – you see I *just* slipped out for a minute, and . . .' stammered Meddle, but after giving him a very hard slap, Aunt Jemima disappeared into the drawing-room and shut the door. Meddle heard the sound of voices.

He remembered the lovely tea. He shot upstairs. He was very dirty and untidy. It took him a long time to get himself clean, brush his hair down well, and change into his other clothes.

'Now I'll go down,' he said, looking at himself in the glass. 'I look very neat and nice. I can hear Mrs. Trottle is still downstairs – Aunt won't say anything horrid to me in front of her, and I'll soon tuck into the cakes.'

So down he went, practising a polite party smile, as he trotted down the stairs. He opened the door and walked in, bowing politely to old Mrs. Trottle, and asking her how she was.

'Oh – there you are at last, Meddle,' said his aunt. 'Well, all the tea-things are stacked up in the kitchen, ready for you to wash. You can go and do them now!'

Well, well, well – what a shock for Meddle. He found himself out in the cold kitchen, faced by an enormous pile of dirty cups and saucers and knives and spoons and plates and dishes! He scowled.

'I'll jolly well tuck into the cakes first,' he said. But he couldn't! Aunt Jemima had put them away and locked the cupboard door.

And will you believe it, when he had washed up and went upstairs gloomily to fetch his sweets to

eat, his aunt's old dog had been there first! Not a
sweet was left in the bag.

But Aunt Jemima wouldn't scold the dog. 'All
these things have happened because you were stu-
pid and disobedient, Meddle,' she said. 'In fact, the
only clever thing you did was to pick your own
house to come to when you were lost.'

'It wasn't clever,' said poor Meddle, felling very
miserable indeed. 'It was just about the SILLIEST
thing I could have done. And if ever I lose myself
in a fog again I'll be jolly careful I don't get lost
exactly outside my own house!'

7: *Meddle Tries to Help*

Meddle got up feeling very happy one morning. He sang so loudly in his bath that his Aunt Jemima rapped on the door.

'Meddle! Do stop that dreadful noise. You've frightened the cat out of the house.'

'What dreadful noise?' said Meddle, surprised. 'I was only singing because I feel good and happy this lovely morning.'

'Oh, dear,' said aunt. 'That means you'll want to help everyone and interfere with everything. I know you, Meddle! Anyway, stop that singing, or whatever it is.'

Meddle came down to breakfast, beaming. 'Now, you tell me anything you want done today,' he said to his aunt. 'I'll do it with pleasure.'

'I don't want your help, thank you,' said Aunt Jemima. 'Last time you helped me you said you'd weed the garden – and you went and pulled up all the little seedlings instead of the weeds. I don't want any more of your help.'

'Well, Aunt – it's not good of you to stop somebody when they want to do a kindness,' said Meddle, offended.

'All right, do your kindness – but go and offer it to someone else, not me,' said his aunt. 'What about old Dame Grumble? She's hurt one of her feet and can't do her shopping properly. Go and offer to do it for her.'

'I don't like Dame Grumble very much,' said Meddle. 'She's got a sharp tongue.'

'So have I,' said his aunt, 'and I shall use it in a minute if you don't stop putting marmalade on your porridge, Meddle.'

'Oh, dear – I thought I was putting on golden syrup,' said Meddle. 'Well – I'll go and see if Dame Grumble wants any errands running – but I hope she doesn't.'

Off he went round to Dame Grumble's little cottage after breakfast. He found her hobbling about her kitchen, grumbling hard to her old black cat.

'I've a good mind to send you away, Blackie! There you sit, as lazy as anything, and let the mice run all round you at night – and you put yourself in my way so that I fall over you and hurt my foot! And now I've got to go out shopping, and hobble along in pain. For shame, Blackie.'

Blackie took no notice at all, but washed herself all over very carefully. Meddle rapped on the door and Dame Grumble called loudly:

'Come in, come in, don't stand there knocking and knocking. Can't you bring the washing in and put it down on the table for me as usual?'

'No,' said Meddle, stepping inside. 'I'm not the washerwoman. I'm Meddle.'

'And what have *you* come bothering me for?'

asked Dame Grumble. 'Bless the fellow, he's gone and trodden on the cat, already!'

'Well, it shouldn't sit down on a black rug,' said Meddle. 'A black cat should have the sense to sit on a white one. Look how she's scratched me! And all I came for was to ask you if I could do your shopping for you. This is a fine reward for kindness, I must say – a long scratch all down my leg.'

'Pooh – that's nothing,' said Dame Grumble. 'Fancy making a fuss about that. Yes, you can do my errands for me. That's certainly kind of you.'

'What would you like me to do?' asked Meddle, getting as far away from the cat as he could.

'I'd like you to fetch my dog for me,' said Dame

68

Grumble. 'He's at the vet's – the animal doctor, you know. And I want my dress back from the cleaner's.'

'Well – I don't know about getting your dog,' said Meddle, nervously. 'Is he fierce at all?'

'No, he's a lamb,' said Dame Grumble. 'He's a a pet. He never even growls, he's so good-tempered. You can take his lead with you, and he'll follow close to your heel without any trouble at all.'

Well, this sounded all right to Meddle. He felt he could manage a dog like that. 'What about your dress?' he asked.

'That should be quite ready,' said Dame Grumble. 'Here's the ticket for it – it's white with a black collar. And I'll just scribble a note for the vet about the dog. His name is Patch, and he's brown with spots on his back. There you are – you can't possibly make a mistake.'

Meddle put one ticket in his left-hand pocket and one in his right. 'Now I shan't mix them up,' he said. 'Well, good-bye, Dame Grumble. I'll soon be back with your dog and your dress.'

He went off down the road to the vet's. He couldn't make himself heard at the front door, so he went round to the yard where there were cages of dogs of all kinds. They set up a great barking when they saw Meddle.

A worried-looking kennel-maid looked round a corner to see what the matter was. 'What do you want?' she said. 'Have you come to fetch a dog?'

'Yes,' said Meddle. 'I want Dame Grumble's dog.'

'What is he like?' asked the girl. 'Could you take him out of his cage yourself, please? I've got a hurt dog here and I can't leave him for a bit.'

'That's all right,' said Meddle, and he fished a bit of paper out of his pocket. 'I've got a description of the dog here. He's white with a black collar. I'll have a look round and see if I can spot him.'

He looked in all the cages. He couldn't see a dog with a white coat and black collar. But at last he came to a very big cage and inside was a grey-white dog wearing a black collar. It was rather a big dog, and Meddle didn't really like the look of it.

'Still, Dame Grumble said it was as quiet as a lamb, and a real pet,' he thought to himself. 'Come along, Patch. Good dog, then, nice dog.'

The dog seemed surprised at Meddle, and even more surprised when his door was opened and he was let out. Meddle snapped the lead on to the big dog's collar.

'Come along,' he said. 'Home, doggy, home!'

The dog growled. Meddle was startled. 'Oh, naughty!' he said. 'Your mistress said you never growled. Come along now!'

He dragged the dog out of the yard, calling good-bye to the kennel-maid as he went. Out of the gate he walked, the dog dragging behind him.

'You're not as well-behaved as your mistress said you were,' said Meddle, and pulled hard at the lead. 'Do you want your head pulled off, silly? I tell you, if it's to be a tug-of-war between us, you won't like it!'

The dog growled so fiercely that Meddle felt alarmed. It sat down hard and Meddle began to despair of ever getting it home. Then he had a bright idea. He saw the butcher's nearby, and felt pleased. 'I'll just tie you to the railings here for a minute,' he told the dog, 'then I'll slip over to the butcher's and buy a big bone. You'll come after me quickly enough then!'

He went to buy a bone. As soon as he came back

72

the dog wagged his tail at him and tried to jump at the bone. Meddle stuffed it into his pocket. 'Now, you just follow me quietly, smelling your bone all the way,' he said. 'And maybe I'll give it to you when we get home.'

The dog trotted after him, jumping at Meddle's pocket and tearing it. Meddle was annoyed. He smacked the dog, which at once showed its teeth in a very alarming manner.

'Here's the cleaners,' said Meddle, relieved. He tied the dog to the fence nearby and disappared into the shop. He pulled out the other bit of paper from his second pocket.

'I've come for a dress sent to be cleaned for Dame Grumble,' he said. 'It's – let me see – it's brown with spots on the back.'

'I haven't a brown dress with spots on the back,' said the girl. 'I've a brown dress without spots, though. That must be the one. I expect it was sent to have the spots cleaned off the back.'

'Oh, yes – I expect it was,' said Meddle. 'Can I take it please? I'm in a hurry. I've got a dog waiting outside.'

'You certainly have,' said the girl. 'He's howling the place down. My word – doesn't he look fierce, too?'

'He does rather,' said Meddle, his heart sinking at the sight of the very angry dog. It was almost pulling the fence down in its antics.

'Come on, Patch. We haven't far to go now,' said Meddle, and took the lead again. The dog at

once smelt the bone in his pocket and jumped at him. Meddle sat down heavily in a puddle, and dropped the brown dress in the mud. He beat off the dog and got up, very angry indeed.

'Look what you've done – messed up a nice clean frock belonging to your mistress!' he scolded the dog.

The dog looked as if it was about to knock him over again, so Meddle hastily took the bone out of his pocket and gave it to him. The dog snatched at it and wanted to sit down and eat it straight away. 'No, you come along home,' said Meddle, pulling hard. 'I'm tired of you. Come along.'

Soon a few more dogs joined them, smelling the bone that the big dog carried. Meddle was really frightened. Oh, dear – it looked as if there would be a fine old dog-fight soon. Dame Grumble's dog was growling without stopping now.

Then a woman called out from over the road in a very angry voice: 'Hey, you! What are you doing with my dog?'

'Which dog's yours?' shouted back Meddle. 'Call him! *I* don't want all these tiresome animals round me. Call him off.'

'I'll tell a policeman, you robber!' cried the woman. 'Stealing dogs like that!'

Meddle went off, scowling, dragging the big dog behind him with even more difficulty. Six other dogs followed in delight sniffing the delicious bone that the big dog carried.

Poor Meddle was very, very thankful when he reached Dame Grumble's house. He dragged the dog into the kitchen and shut the door.

The dog saw the cat and immediately flew at it. Blackie tore up the grandfather clock and sat there on the top, spitting with rage. The dog jumped at the clock and brought it down with a tremendous crash. The cat leapt to the top of the curtains, Meddle almost jumped out of his skin, and the dog fled under the table in fright.

Dame Grumble came rushing in from the garden. 'What's all this? What's the matter with Blackie? What was that crash? Oh, my beautiful clock! Who knocked it over?'

'Your horrible, snarling, bad-tempered dog,' said Meddle, in a very bad temper himself now. 'Take your nasty animal – and your dress! I've had enough of doing errands for you!'

He flung the muddy dress on the table and turned to go. 'Oh,' cried Dame Grumble, 'what a dirty dress – and it isn't even mine! Mine was white with a black collar. I told you so!'

At that moment the dog appeared from under the table. Dame Grumble gave a scream. 'What's this dog doing here? He's not mine! What a horrible creature! Mine was brown with spots down his back. I told you so. I even wrote everything down so that you couldn't make a mistake.'

Meddle stared at Dame Grumble and felt himself going wobbly at the legs. He looked at the dog and then he looked at the dress. He'd mixed them up – the dog should have been brown with black spots, not the dress; and the dress should have been white with a black collar, not the dog. Oh, dear, oh, dear – now what was he to do?

He crept to the door. He opened it, but before he could escape out of the front gate he marched straight into a big policeman, who was followed by the angry woman who had shouted at him in the street.

The policeman caught hold of his arm. 'I want to know where the dog is that you stole from the

kennels,' he said sternly. 'It's been reported to me. Where's that dog?'

'I didn't steal it. It was all a mistake,' said Meddle. The dog appeared at the door and saw its mistress. It rushed to her with whines of delight. Then Dame Grumble appeared and began to talk so loudly to the policeman that Meddle was able to escape. He rushed thankfully back to his Aunt Jemima's and put himself to bed, out of everybody's way.

But that wasn't a bit of good. Dame Grumble, the policeman, the woman and the dog, all came to his aunt's house, and before poor Meddle could even hide in the wardrobe there they were all round his bed!

Now he's got to pay for the grandfather clock being mended, and pay a fine for getting the wrong dog, and pay for the wrong brown dress to be cleaned all over again for its rightful owner. He won't have any pocket-money for a very long time. Poor Meddle.

'That will teach you not to meddle and muddle as you do,' said Aunt Jemima. But it won't. He just can't help it, can he?

8: *Mister Meddle in a Fix*

Mister Meddle arrived at his Aunt Jemima's hopping she would let him stay for a day or two. He had spent all his money, and he thought it would be such a good idea if he could live with his aunt for a little while.

'Good gracious – so *you've* turned up again!' said Aunt Jemima, in disgust, as Meddle came walking in at the door. 'Talk about a bed penny!'

'I don't know what you mean, Aunt,' said Meddle, surprised. 'I've come to see if I can be any help to you.'

'You can stay and have lunch with me if you go and fetch some parcels and packages I've left at the shops,' said Aunt Jemima. 'But you will leave immediately after dinner, Meddle – no staying on for weeks as you did last time.'

'Are there *many* parcels?' asked Meddle. He didn't like carrying a heavy load.

'Plenty,' said Aunt Jemima. 'There's a chair that's been mended – and a sack of carrots – and the kitchen clock – and a whole pile of smaller ones, too. I went to fetch them yesterday, but my little car broke down and I had to leave it at the garage to be seen to.'

'Is it mended yet?' asked Meddle, hopefully.

'It may be,' said his aunt. 'You can call in and see if you like – and run it home for me – but DON'T knock too many lamp-posts down on the way. They are expensive things to pay for. Unless, of course, you are feeling rather rich, Meddle, and don't mind.'

'I'm not feeling rich at all,' said Meddle, thinking of his empty pockets. 'Not in the least. I'll fetch your little car and all your parcels, Aunt, and I'll be back again in a jiffy.'

'I know your jiffies!' said his aunt. 'More like five or six hours! Well – I shan't wait for lunch, so just hurry up. Here is the list of shops I've left my parcels at. And if you want to pay for them, give them the money and I'll pay you when you come back.'

Meddle walked off. 'Pay for her parcels! I should think not!' he said to himself. 'For one thing I can't, and for another thing if I did do such a silly thing, Aunt Jemima *wouldn't* pay me back – she'd say I owed her money, anyway, which I suppose I do.'

He went to the garage first. Ah, his aunt's car was ready. Good. Meddle rather fancied himself driving a car, and he got into the driving-seat at once. Off he went at top speed, nearly taking a petrol pump with him.

He came to the chair-mender's and collected the chair, all neatly wrapped up in sacking. The man didn't ask for payment, so that was lucky. Meddle put the chair in at the back of the car. Then he

drove to the greengrocer's and got the sack of carrots.

'Fifty pence, please,' said the man, when he had put the carrots in at the back.

'Certainly,' said Meddle. 'Send the bill in to my aunt,' and he drove off before the man could take the carrots back again.

He got the kitchen clock, too, done up nicely in a cardboard box, marked 'This Way Up.' Not that Meddle took any notice of that at all. The clock had to stand on its head on the back seat.

It didn't like it at all, and began to strike very loudly indeed.

'All right, all right – don't keep telling me you

are mended!' said Meddle. 'Be quiet!'

The smaller parcels had been left at the grocer's. There were a great many. 'I'll just take them out to my car now,' said Meddle, grandly.

'Certainly. That will be one pound, and thirty-four pence, please,' said the shop-woman, politely.

'Send in the bill,' said Meddle, picking up the parcels.

'Your Aunt Jemima always pays when she takes the things,' said the shop-woman firmly. 'I'd like the money, please.'

'Aunt Jemima will send it,' said Meddle, just as firmly, taking a step towards the door.

'Put those parcels down,' said the woman, suddenly angry. 'No money, no parcels!'

Meddle felt annoyed. Was he going to lose his nice lunch at his aunt's because of this exasperating woman? He really didn't know what to do.

Then the telephone bell rang and the woman hurried to the back of the shop to answer it. 'I'll be back in a moment,' she called to Meddle.

'Ah!' thought Meddle, 'now's my chance! I'll slip these things straight out to the car and be off before she has finished telephoning!'

He rushed out of the shop with the parcels swinging all round him. He ran to one of the cars outside, wrenched open the door and flung the parcels on to the back seat, hoping there would be room for them.

He slammed the door, and started up the engine. There was no sign of the shop-woman. Good – he would race off home straight away.

Off he went. He turned the corner, and sat back in glee. Good – he had all the parcels safely, he hadn't had to pay for any, and he got Aunt Jemima's car back for her. She ought to be so pleased with him that she would let him stay at least a day or two, not just for lunch only.

'Toot-toot, parp-parp!' said a car loudly, behind him. Meddle looked back. He caught sight of an extremely angry face – a very fierce face indeed.

'What's the matter with *him*?' thought Meddle, alarmed. 'What's he hooting at me for? I haven't broken any road rules.'

84

'Toot-toot, parp-parp!' went the car, trying to catch up Meddle.

Meddle decided to go faster. He didn't at all like the look of that man in the car. He might be a robber of some sort. This was a very lonely road he was on – suppose the man got in front of him, and forced him into the hedge! He would be able to rob Meddle of all the parcels he had so carefully fetched!

So he went faster than ever, and the hedge spun past so quickly that it seemed just a green line and nothing more. The car rocked about dangerously – and still from behind came that angry, insistent hooting!

Meddle was sure that the man at the wheel was shaking his fist at him.

'Either a robber or quite mad,' thought Meddle, bouncing so hard in a rut that he almost fell over the side of the car. 'Well, well – I must say that my aunt's car is a very good one – much faster than I expected. Thank goodness it is faster than that robber's behind.'

Meddle shook off the man at last, tore down a side-street and came to a stop outside his aunt's house. No sign of that man, thank goodness. He pulled out all the parcels and staggered into the house with them. 'I'm back, Aunt,' he said. 'And here are all your parcels. Haven't I been quick? I got your car, too.'

'Well, that's splendid,' said his aunt, pleased. 'Undo the chair, will you? We need another. And put the kitchen clock on the mantelpiece. And you might get a few carrots out of the sack and I'll cook them for our lunch.'

Meddle began undoing the big parcels. Where was the mended chair? Funny – he couldn't seem to see it.

Meddle undid a large parcel and to his astonishment out came a wash-tub. He hadn't remembered collecting a wash-tub.

'Where did *that* come from?' said his aunt in surprise. 'I never bought a wash-tub. And where *is* that mended chair? And do get the clock out, Meddle, I want to know the time.'

'You'll soon know it,' said Meddle, unpacking at top speed. 'It stood on the back seat and struck without stopping when I put it there.'

He unpacked a parrot-cage and a lamp-shade, an electric iron and a dog-basket. Aunt Jemima stared at everything in amazement.

'Where *did* you get these? Where's my chair and clock and carrots?' she asked.

'I can't imagine,' said Meddle, in a panic. 'The carrots were in a sack, and the clock struck, so I *know* it was there, and the legs of the chair stuck out, so I'm sure I fetched that. Oh, Aunt – there's been some very queer magic at work here!'

'Is there anything left in the car?' asked his aunt. Meddle was just going to say 'no' when there came a knock at the door.

Meddle went to answer it. Mr. Plod the policeman stood there!

'Little question of the car outside,' said Mr. Plod. 'It's been reported to me as stolen. Do you know how it got there?'

Meddle stared at the car he had left outside. 'That's my Aunt Jemima's car,' he said. 'Don't be silly, policeman.'

'Ho! We'll soon see who's silly,' said Mr. Plod. 'See that car's number? Well, it's the same as the one that belongs to Mr. Grim, and it was stolen this morning. See?'

Meddle didn't see. He called loudly to his aunt. 'Aunt Jemima! Do come, please, and tell the policeman this is your car. He says it's been stolen.'

Aunt Jemima came rushing out. She stared at

the car, and then she stared at Meddle. 'Where's *my* car?' she cried. 'What have you done with it? That's not my car!'

'Just what I said, Madam,' said Mr. Plod. 'This is one that's been stolen. And what's more, Madam, there were a whole lot of valuable things in it, too – an electric iron, a dog-basket, a wash-tub, a – –'

'Parrot-cage, a lampshade,' went on Aunt Jemima, glaring at poor Meddle. 'Explain this, Meddle – and tell me exactly where *my* things are – especially the kitchen clock.'

Well, Meddle couldn't explain. He couldn't for the life of him think what had happened. Surely it was a bad dream!

'When this fellow came running out of the grocer's with a lot of parcels, what did he do but jump into Mr. Grim's empty car standing by the kerb with a whole lot of others,' said Mr. Plod, 'and away he went at sixty miles an hour! And Mr. Grim jumped into his brother's car and chased him – but he got away.'

'*Meddle!*' said his aunt, amazed and shocked. 'Is *this* the way you behave nowadays?'

'No,' said Meddle, desperately. 'I suppose I – er – well, I just got into the wrong car, Aunt Jemima.'

'Officer,' said Aunt Jemima, turning to the solemn policeman, 'give my apologies to Mr. Grim. Ask him to come here and collect his car and his belongings – and beg him please to stay and have lunch with me so that my nephew can explain his extraordinary behaviour.'

'Very good, Madam,' said Mr. Plod, with a grin, and away he went.

'Go and wash your hands for lunch,' said Aunt Jemima to Meddle. 'I've no doubt Mr. Grim will soon be along.'

Meddle went into the kitchen. A delicious smell of stew came from there – and on the stove he could see some kind of pudding bubbling away.

Meddle didn't wash his hands. He tip-toed through the kitchen, and through the scullery, out of the back door, and down the garden, and then he jumped over the wall at the bottom.

It was a terrible pity, but he really felt he couldn't stay for lunch if Mr. Grim was coming. He went down the lane, hoping he wouldn't meet anyone.

He doesn't know who's coming round the corner, on his way to have lunch with Aunt Jemima, pleased to have been invited. It's Mr. Grim hurrying – longing for a nice meal – longing for a nasty talk with Meddle. Look out, Meddle – you're JUST about to bump into Mr. Grim – there – I knew you would!

9: *Meddle and the Biggle-Gobble*

'Meddle, for goodness' sake, go out for a walk and stop meddling in my cooking,' said Aunt Jemima, crossly. 'You've put salt in the pie instead of sugar, and dropped all the currants on the floor, and ...'

'All right, Aunt, all right. No need to get cross just because I'm helping,' said Meddle, and he reached for his hat. He had just spilt the custard powder, and he thought he had better go out before his aunt discovered that, too. Dear, dear – what a pity people wouldn't let him be kind and help them more!

Meddle had one of his interfering moods on when he felt he could do things very much better than anyone else. He wondered if he should call at the butcher's and tell him how to make bigger sausages. He decided he wouldn't because the butcher had a nasty-looking chopper and might chase him.

'I might, perhaps, go in and tell the baker how to make a much, much richer fruit cake by putting in twice as much raisins and currants,' he said, but when he peeped in at the baker's window he saw that Mrs. Biscuit, the baker's wife, was at the counter that day, instead of the kindly baker himself.

'She's quite likely to throw hard, stale buns at me if I try to help her,' thought Meddle. 'And, what's more, she'd probably hit me every time. No – I won't help the baker today.'

He walked on till he came to Dame Rimminy's cottage. He saw green smoke coming from her chimney, so he knew she was making spells that morning. Ah, now – if he could help *her*, how grateful she would be! He walked up to the door.

It was wide open. Meddle looked inside. There was a small round room, and in the middle of it was a queer fire with green flames. On it hung a black pot out of which green smoke came. Dame Rimminy was making a really fine spell, no doubt about that!

Meddle looked for her. She wasn't there. She was at the bottom of her garden looking for the very earliest snowdrop, which she wanted for her spell.

Meddle tiptoed to the pot. My, my – how it gurgled and bubbled! What spell was Dame Rimminy making?

He caught sight of a big, black book on a nearby table – 'The Big Book of Useful Spells.' Meddle read its title and then looked at the page where the book was opened.

'Ha – A Spell for Making a Biggle-Gobble,' he read out loud. 'Dear me – a *Biggle-Gobble*. What *can* that be? I've never heard of such a thing before. How very, very exciting!'

He read the directions: 'Get the pot boiling till the smoke is green. Now put in one cat's hair, half a spoonful of rice dipped in red ink, one old shoe, two pinches of Glory Powder, and stir with a feathered hat. Chant the following three times, and then wait for five minutes for the Biggle-Gobble to apppear.'

Meddle smiled happily. Why – he could do all that easily! Perhaps if he made the Biggle-Gobble, whatever it was, for Dame Rimminy, she would be so pleased with him that she would give him one of her famous Magic Toffees. You put one in your mouth, and, however much you sucked it, you could never, never suck it all away. Meddle had always longed for a Magic Toffee.

He began to make the spell. 'One cat's hair. Come here, puss. Now, keep still, I only want *one* hair. I'm going to pull. Oh, you horrid cat, you scratched me!'

So she had – but Meddle had some hairs. He dropped one into the pot. Then he found a tin labelled 'RICE' and took out half a spoonful. He found the bottle of red ink in Dame Rimminy's desk, and poured it over the rice. It went bright red immediately.

'Into the pot with you!' said Meddle, and into the pot went the rice dyed red! The pot gave a

sudden gurgle and made Meddle jump. He peered into it. Was the Biggle-Gobble forming already?

'Now to put in one old shoe,' he said, and he looked for one. He saw two shoes belonging to Dame Rimminy standing on the floor. He looked at them. 'Well – they're not new, so I suppose they might be called *old*,' he said.

He picked up one and flung it into the bubbling pot. It almost bubbled over, and a queer snorting noise began to come out of it. Meddle felt rather alarmed. Still – he must certainly go on with the spell now. It was very, very bad to begin a spell and not to finish it.

'Now for two pinches of Glory-Powder,' said

Meddle, and looked all round for it. Ah – there it was, in a tin on the top shelf. He climbed up and got it. He scattered two pinches of the curious yellow powder into the pot.

It jerked and bubbled and snorted as if something alive was in it. Meddle felt quite excited. 'Now I must stir it with a feathered hat and chant the magic words!' he said.

He looked about and saw a fine feathered hat belonging to Dame Rimminy hanging on a peg. Ah! – that was just the thing.

He took it and began to stir the bubbling pot with it, chanting the magic words: 'Chirimmy, chuckadee, lillity-loo, Come Biggle-Gobble, I'm waiting for you, Chirimmy, chuckadee, lillity-loo!'

He threw the wet feathered hat on the floor and waited. Five minutes more and the Biggle-Gobble would appear! Whatever would it be like? Wouldn't Dame Rimminy be pleased to see that he had made the spell for her!

But at that very moment Dame Rimminy came in with a small snowdrop. She glared at Meddle.

'What are *you* here for? You know I don't like anyone here when I'm making a spell. Get out!'

'Oh, but Dame Rimminy – I've been saving you a lot of trouble,' said Meddle, smiling. '*I've* made your spell for you. It will soon be ready!'

'Nonsense!' said Dame Rimminy. 'No one can make a Flyaway Spell except me!'

'A – a *flyaway* spell, did you say?' said Meddle, puzzled. 'But – but I thought you were making a

96

Biggle-Gobble spell!'

'Don't be silly. Who wants a Biggle-Gobble?' said Dame Rimminy.

'Your book was open at that spell,' said poor Meddle. Dame Rimminy stepped over to it. She turned over the page and showed Meddle what was printed there, 'How to Make a Flyaway Spell.'

'The wind blew the page over, that's all,' she said. 'I wasn't going to make a Biggle-Gobble spell. Whatever *would* I do with a hungry Biggle-Gobble!'

'Are they hungry?' said Meddle, edging towards the door, and watching the bubbling pot with great alarm.

'Always hungry,' said Dame Rimminy. Then she caught sight of her feathered hat lying in a puddle on the floor. She pounced on it.

'Meddle! MEDDLE! You haven't been using my best hat to stir the pot with, have you? And where is my other shoe? Have you thrown that in the pot? Come here, Meddle, I'll box both your ears and your nose too, and I'll spank you so that you can't sit down for a week. Come here, Meddle!'

But Meddle was tearing round and round the room, trying to get away from the angry old dame. And all the time the pot kept bubbling and gurgling and snorting. Three minutes had gone – four minutes –

FIVE MINUTES!

BANG! CRASH! SNORT!

97

Out of the pot leapt a Biggle-Gobble. Meddle
stared at it in the greatest alarm. It was rather like
a small dragon, with a round head like a cat's, and
long ears – and far, far too many teeth! It stood
and snorted in the middle of the floor.

'After him, Biggle-Gobble!' shouted Dame
Rimminy. 'After him! If you're hungry, he's the
one to catch!'

Meddle gave a loud yell and leapt straight out
of the window. The Biggle-Gobble leapt out too.
And then, my word, what a wonderful chase there
was! Down the garden and over the wall, along the
street and round the corner, over the stile and

across the field, into the lane and up the hill, along the High Street and helter-skelter for Meddle's Aunt Jemima!

The Biggle-Gobble thoroughly enjoyed it. But Meddle didn't. His heart beat so fast and he panted so loudly that he really frightened himself. Why, oh, why, had he meddled in that spell, and made a Biggle-Gobble!

He rushed into his aunt's house – but before he could bang on the door the Biggle Gobble was in the hall too. Aunt Jemima heard the noise and came out of the kitchen in surprise. When she saw the Biggle-Gobble she gave a shriek.

'A Biggle-Gobble! How *dare* you bring one home, Meddle! He'll eat everything! They're always hungry!'

'Don't let him eat me, don't let him,' wailed Meddle, and dived behind the sofa.

'Where did he come from?' demanded Aunt Jemima, flapping at the Biggle-Gobble with a newspaper, just as if it were a wasp.

'From Dame Rimminy's,' sobbed poor Meddle.

'I'll telephone to her at once and tell her to come and take it away,' said Aunt Jemima. 'Oh, my goodness, it's eating up all my new cakes. Shoo, you greedy creature, shoo!'

She went to the telephone and rang up Dame Rimminy. 'What do you want to go making Biggle-Gobbles for? One has chased Meddle and it's eating my cakes. *What's* that you say? *Meddle* made it? It's *his* Biggle-Gobble, and he can keep it? But,

I tell you, it's in my house and won't go away. I *won't* keep it!'

She slammed down the telephone receiver and glared at the Biggle-Gobble, who was now eating a pie. 'Stop that!' she shouted. 'Go and nibble Meddle's toes. Go and nibble his red ears.'

'No, no, Aunt,' wailed Meddle, and fled out of the door in fright. The Biggle-Gobble followed him at once. Aunt Jemima shut the door with a bang and bolted it. Then she fastened all the windows. Meddle could play about with the Biggle-Gobble all he liked – it wasn't coming back *here*!

The Biggle-Gobble gave Meddle a nip with its sharp teeth, but it didn't like the taste of him. So it trotted off to somebody's dustbin, took the lid off and began to gobble up potato peel. Meddle slid round the corner and ran off at top speed.

He went back to his aunt's at sixty miles an hour, climbed up the tree outside his window, and broke the glass to get in. His Aunt Jemima was very angry, and chased him up and down stairs just like the Biggle-Gobble – except that she had a very nasty walking-stick in her hand.

Poor Meddle. He is afraid to go out of the house in case he meets the Biggle-Gobble, so he's got to stay indoors and scrub and wash and polish until his arms are ready to drop off.

'I'll never meddle with spells again,' he says. 'That awful Biggle-Gobble! I do hope it isn't still waiting for me round the corner.'

It isn't. It went back to Dame Rimminy and she

gave it a good meal of dog biscuits and milk, and it curled up by the fire and went to sleep, purring. She sold it to the Green witch for three golden pounds, because the witch had too many mice and the Biggle-Gobble was really a wonderful mouser.

But Meddle doesn't know that. He thinks it's still looking for him!

10: *Meddle Goes Shopping*

One day Meddle went to see his Aunt Jemima. He had been keeping away from her for some time because she wasn't at all pleased with his meddling ways.

He found a note on the back door.

'Baker. One loaf, please.'

'Milkman. One pint, please.'

'Laundry. Look in scullery.'

'Dear me!' thought Meddle. 'Aunt Jemima

must be out, or else she's ill in bed. I'll go in and see.'

So he pushed open the kitchen door and in he went. No one seemed to be about. Meddle went to the larder door and opened it. Ooooh! Jam-tarts on a plate. He was just about to take one when a voice made him jump.

'If that's the baker, leave a cake, too!'

'It isn't the baker. It's me, Meddle,' called Meddle. 'Where are you, Aunt Jemima?'

'I've got a chill and I'm in bed,' said the voice, rather croakily. 'Come up and see me. And DON'T snoop round the larder, Meddle. I know exactly how many jam-tarts there are.'

Meddle frowned, shut the larder door softly, and went upstairs. His aunt was in bed with an enormous night-cap on, and a great array of medicine bottles by her side.

'Poor Aunt Jemima! Can I do anything for you?' asked Meddle. 'Shall I give you your medicine? You do look ill.'

'I feel it,' groaned his aunt. 'Yes, give me my medicine. It's in the blue bottle.'

Meddle got the bottle. 'How much do I pour you?' he asked.

'A tablespoonful,' said his aunt, lying with her eyes shut, looking very miserable indeed. Meddle poured out the medicine into a tablespoon. Then he held it out. 'Sit up, Aunt Jemima. Here's your medicine.'

She sat up, and Meddle held the spoon to her

mouth. But as soon as she tasted it she gave a loud yell and knocked the spoon out of Meddle's hand. The medicine went all over him.

'Meddle! What's that? That isn't my nice, sweet cough medicine. It's HORRIBLE!'

'Well, you said the blue bottle,' said Meddle, holding it up. His aunt groaned, and lay down again.

'That's my eye-drops. You *would* get the wrong bottle! Couldn't you even look to see what the label says as plain as can be – EYE-DROPS.'

'I'm sorry, Aunt,' said Meddle, picking up another blue bottle. 'I'll give you the right medicine this time.'

'No, you won't. You won't give me anything at all, if I can help it,' said his aunt. 'All I want you to do is to go away as quickly as possible before you start meddling. Go home, Meddle, go home!'

'You sound as if I were a dog!' said Meddle indignantly. 'Please, Aunt, isn't there *anything* I can do? Don't you want any shopping done, for instance?'

'Yes, I do,' said his aunt, shutting her eyes again. 'But *you're* not going to do it, Meddle! I know what your shopping is like. Even if you take a list with you you always bring the wrong things back. Meddle and muddle, that's what you do! Go home!'

Meddle was very hurt. He went down the stairs and into the scullery. A voice followed him. 'And don't forget that the larder door squeaks, Meddle!

I know when anyone is opening it!'

Meddle thought his aunt was very horrid. He wished he could show her she was wrong about him. Didn't he want to be helpful? Yes, he did! Then why wouldn't she let him at least do her shopping?

His eye caught sight of a list on the kitchen table. Ah! This must be Aunt Jemima's shopping list. Maybe she had just been going out shopping when she had fallen ill. Well, what about Mister Meddle taking the list, doing the shopping simply beautifully, and showing his Aunt Jemima that he really was a clever fellow after all?

He put his hand into his pocket. Had he got any money with him that morning? Yes, he had. His uncle had sent him quite a lot for his birthday the week before. Should he go shopping with his own money and get it back from his aunt afterwards – or should he go back upstairs and ask her for some shopping money?

'No. She wouldn't give me any – and she would still say I wasn't to do the shopping,' said Meddle to himself. 'I'll use my own – and when I come back with all the things on the list, she'll be so pleased with me that she'll give me a few extra pence for my trouble, as well as the money I have spent.'

He picked up the neat little list and went out of the house. He looked at the list as he went.

'One small blue table-cloth. Well, that's easy. I know just the kind she has! One tea-cloth. That's easy too. I can get it at the same shop. One white apron. Lucky I know the kind she wears in the morning! I'll have to get a nice big size for Aunt Jemima because she's rather fat. I'll go to the draper's for all these.'

He looked at the list again. 'One sheet. One pillow-case. One Turkish towel, small. Well, well – this is really quite a bit of luck. I can do all the shopping at the same shop! I'm sure the draper will sell all these.'

Meddle was pleased. This was very easy shopping to do. He hoped he had enough money.

He went to the draper's and walked to the

counter that sold towels and sheets and pillow-cases.

'I want a nice white sheet, please, for a single bed, and a pillow-case to match, and a small Turkish towel,' said Meddle.

'Only *one* sheet, sir?' asked the shop-girl. 'We usually sell them in pairs.'

'Well, my aunt only wants *one*,' said Meddle, firmly. 'So one it must be.'

The shop-girl managed to find an odd sheet, a plain pillow-case and a small Turkish towel.

'Anything else?' she asked.

'Oh, yes. One small blue table-cloth, one tea-cloth and a white apron, large size,' said Meddle, looking at his list. 'That's all. I'll take them with me.'

He had them wrapped up, and the girl gave him the bill. Oh dear – it took nearly all the money his uncle had sent him for his birthday. Never mind – Aunt Jemima would repay it all.

He went out of the shop, pleased with himself. Now Aunt Jemima would see how clever he could be at shopping! He was sure that he had got just the right things.

He went back to the house and let himself in at the back door.

Somebody else was there, too – the young man from the laundry. He was collecting the basket of washing.

'Good morning,' he said to Meddle. 'I've come for the laundry – but I can't find the washing-list.

Have you seen it?'

'No, I haven't,' said Meddle. The young man went to the bottom of the stairs and called loudly.

'Your nephew is here, Mam, and *he* can't find the washing-list either. So I'll just take the washing without it, and make out a list for you myself.'

'Thank you,' called back Aunt Jemima, croakily. The young man went out and shut the door, carrying the basket on his shoulder. Meddle ran upstairs with his parcel, beaming all over his face.

'Aunt Jemima, I found your shopping list and I've been shopping for you! Look!'

'What *do* you mean?' said his aunt, amazed. Meddle undid the parcel in great haste, anxious to

show all the things he had bought.

'One sheet. One table-cloth, blue. One apron. One tea-cloth. One Turkish towel. One pillow-case. There you are – and here's the bill. Now, don't say I make a muddle whenever I go shopping!'

Aunt Jemima stared at the things in astonishment. 'But why did you buy all these?' she said. 'I don't want them!'

'Well, they were on your shopping list downstairs!' said Meddle, and he pushed the list into his aunt's hands. 'See – they're all down there.'

'Meddle,' said his aunt, 'Meddle, are you *quite* mad? This is the *laundry* list – the list of things I was sending to be washed. No wonder the man couldn't find it. Is there any sense in taking a *washing* list and going out to *buy* all the things on it?'

'Oh, Aunt – I thought it was your shopping list!' wailed Meddle. 'I did really. Please pay me back for all I've bought.'

'Certainly not,' said his aunt. 'Take them home yourself and use them – and tie the apron round your waist when you do your washing-up! You'll look fine! Go home, Meddle. If you don't, I'll get up and take the broom to you!'

So now Meddle is going home with all the things he bought, because the shop won't take them back. He's very sad – he has wasted his money, and made such a muddle again. He never *will* learn not to meddle, will he?

11: *Now, Mister Meddle!*

Just over the farmer's fence was a fine big plum tree, full of ripe purple plums. The boys of the village knew this tree well, and each summer they came along to try to get the plums.

They had to keep a good look out for the farmer and his dog. Once two boys had been caught and the farmer had whipped them well, which served them right. Now they didn't dare to get over the fence into the field. They just tried to knock down the plums that hung above the fence.

'Come on – throw stones up, or bits of wood,' said Harry, picking up a big stone. He threw it into the plum tree, and knocked down a plum. It also broke a small branch, which fell into the road.

'Pity that branch hasn't got plums on!' said Jack. 'I say – that's an idea – let's throw up something to break the branches – then maybe we'll get a lot of plums at once if the branches fall down our side.'

Leonard went to get some walking-sticks from his home nearby. Soon the boys were flinging up the sticks and breaking the smaller, very brittle branches easily. Down they came, some with plums on them.

Now Mister Meddle happened to come along the

road just about then. Of course, when he saw the little crowd of boys with sticks, he went up at once. He loved to meddle in anything.

'Ha! That's a silly thing to do, to try to pick plums by throwing sticks!' said Meddle. 'Why don't you be sensible, and climb the tree?'

'We're afraid to,' said Jack, thinking of the farmer and his dog.

'What! A great boy like you afraid of climbing a tree!' said Meddle. 'Good gracious! When *I* was a boy I always climbed trees. *I* wasn't afraid! I could climb that tree in two shakes of a duck's tail!'

Harry winked at the others. 'You couldn't!' he said. 'I bet you you couldn't!'

'I'll just show you then!' said Meddle. 'And what's more, I'll pick the plums for you so that you don't damage the tree any more. Now see how well *I* can shin up this plum tree!'

He climbed over the fence, and shinned up the plum tree. The boys pretended to admire him, and shouted loudly, 'Jolly good, Mister Meddle! Fine! You went up in a trice! Are there any plums near you?'

'*I'll* show you how to pick plums!' said Meddle, and he began to throw some down to the boys. They picked them up in glee and filled their pockets. Silly old Meddle – what a thing to do!

Suddenly Meddle noticed that the boys were no longer there. He looked down in surprise. Where had they gone, all of a sudden?

The boys had certainly gone – gone at top speed

too – but somebody else was there, under the tree, somebody with an extremely fierce-looking dog!

'Oh – er – good morning, Farmer Straw,' said Meddle, peering between the boughs. 'Er – can I throw you down some plums?'

'Mr. Meddle, I'm surprised at you!' said Farmer Straw, in his loud voice. 'Yes, downright surprised at you! Climbing my plum tree and throwing my plums down! What do you mean by it?'

'Nothing,' said Meddle. 'I was merely showing some boys how to pick plums without damaging the tree. You ought to thank me for saving your tree from having its branches broken off by sticks and stones! You ought to give me a reward.'

'Ho! Well, you come on down here and I'll give you a *fine* reward,' said Farmer Straw, in a roaring kind of voice. 'Come along! You'll have a reward all right. Always meddling in something, aren't you? I suppose it didn't occur to you that the *quickest* way of saving my tree and its plums would be to drive those boys off? Come on down and have your reward.'

Meddle didn't want to. He didn't like the look of the dog or of the farmer either. He didn't think he would even like the reward, whatever it was. In

fact, he thought he would prefer to sit up in the tree the whole of the day rather than go near that most unpleasant-looking dog!

'Well, well! I haven't hours to waste on you, Meddle,' said the farmer. 'I'll leave you here.'

Meddle heaved a sigh of relief when he saw the farmer striding off. He began to climb down the tree. A horrible growl stopped him, and he climbed up again at top speed.

The farmer had gone – but the dog hadn't! 'Grrr-rrr-rrr!' said the dog. 'Meddle by name and Meddle by nature! Just come down and meddle with me. Grrr-rr-rr!'

But Meddle wasn't going to meddle with a snarling dog – so goodness knows *how* long he'll stay up in that plum tree!

12: *A Surprise for Mister Meddle*

Mister Meddle was always meddling in things that were no business of his, and poking his nose in where he wasn't wanted.

But he got a great surprise when he went to stay with his cousins, Snip and Snap. They didn't like meddlers, they didn't like borrowers, and they got very impatient indeed with their cousin Meddle.

'Who's taken my new whipping top?' said Snip. 'You, Meddle? Well, where is it then? Where have you put it?'

'Dear me – I'm sure I put it back on the shelf,' said Meddle. But it wasn't there, of course.

'Meddle! Did you borrow my watch?' asked Snap. 'I can't find it anywhere.'

'Dear me – yes, I did,' said Meddle, looking at his wrist. 'I wanted to be sure of catching my bus, you know. Oh, Snap – I'm sorry, but it must have slipped off my wrist.'

'Meddle, did you go and give the cat that milk pudding out of the larder?' called his Aunt Amanda. 'Or did you eat it yourself?'

'Oh, Aunt, the cat mewed so loudly and was so hungry I thought you'd *want* me to give it some-

thing to eat,' said Meddle. 'And I don't much like milk pudding.'

'Well, other people do,' said his aunt, crossly. 'Snip and Snap – you'll have to deal with Meddle for me. If he meddles much more I'll send him away!'

'If you take our things again and lose them or don't bring them back we'll use magic on *your* things – and we'll make them disappear!' said Snip to Meddle.

'Pooh!' said Meddle. 'You're only kids. You don't know any magic. You ought to be *pleased* when I bother myself with your things.'

'Well, we're not,' said Snap. 'Now remember, Meddle – the very next time you meddle with our things, we shall meddle with yours – and away they'll go under your very nose!'

Meddle didn't believe Snip and Snap. He took no notice of their threats at all. He just went on doing what he liked. He borrowed their ball to play with and it fell into a gutter on the roof of the house and couldn't be got down. He borrowed Snap's new socks and because they were too small he wore them into holes.

'He's hopeless,' said Snip to Snap. 'We'll have to teach him a lesson. What about our wonderful Disappearing Trick?'

'Oooh, yes,' said Snap. 'We'll get our friends in to help. Let's call a meeting. We'll ask Tippy, Jinky, Impy and Heyho.'

So all those four met with Snip and Snap at Tippy's and talked about how to punish Meddle for his aggravating ways.

'We'll do the Disappearing Trick on him,' said Snip. 'We'll get his football, his cricket bat, his new pair of stockings and his football boots. We'll tie long, long black thread to them, and tie the other ends to your bicycles.'

Snap began to giggle as he saw the surprised faces of the others.

'It's all right, we're not mad,' he said. 'It's a trick we've played before. Now you, Tippy, can have the stockings tied to your bicycle. The black thread will be very long indeed, and won't be seen – so a

ong time after you've passed by on your bicycle
the stockings will come dragging along the road,
looking as if they're coming all by themselves.
You'll be out of sight, you see!'

Tippy laughed loudly. 'My, what a good trick!
And I suppose you'll tie the other things to the
other bicycles, and they'll come along the road,
too!'

'Yes – we'll tie the boots to Jinky's bicycle, the
football to Impy's and the cricket bat to Heyho's,'
grinned Snip. 'You'll ride by one after another,
you see, and Meddle won't *dream* that anything is
tied to you. The stockings will come wriggling
along like snakes, the boots will come jiggling by,

the football will bounce along all by itself and the cricket bat will race along like anything.'

Everyone began to laugh. Impy held his sides. 'My, this is the best joke I've ever heard of. When do we play it?'

'This evening,' said Snap. 'We'll get you the stockings and all the other things this afternoon when Meddle is out, and we'll give you reels of black thread, too. You can each tie your things on and then go to the little shed at the end of Jiminy Lane.'

'You'll see us walking by with Meddle,' said Snip. 'And that will be your signal to set out – one by one, mind, with about a minute's time between each. Leave us to do the rest!'

'I shall fall off my bicycle with laughing,' said Impy. 'I know I shall.'

'I'd love to see Meddle's face when his football comes bouncing by on its own!' said Jinky.

Everyone went home, giggling. What a trick! Whatever would Meddle say?

Now, that evening, when everything was ready and prepared, Snip and Snap went to Meddle.

'Have you found my watch?' demanded Snap.

'What about my ball?' said Snip.

'Oh, go away,' said Meddle, crossly. 'You know I haven't found them. Leave me alone. I'm going for my evening walk and I don't want you.'

But Snip and Snap went with him. They went down the lane, and passed the little shed. Inside were Tippy, Jinky, Impy and Heyho waiting

npatiently with their bicycles. Tied to the backs
f them with long black thread were all the things
elonging to Meddle!

'Meddle, we're going to teach you a lesson,' said
nip, solemnly. 'We're going to work some magic
ere tonight, and send away some of the things you
ke best – things belonging to *you*!'

'Oh, don't be silly,' said Meddle. 'Go home! As
you knew any magic!'

'Meddle,' said Snap, in such a peculiar voice
hat Meddle stopped, startled. 'Meddle! Would
ou like to see your new stockings, your football
oots, your football and your cricket bat all dis-
ppear?'

'Don't talk nonsense,' said Meddle, uneasily. 'And let me tell you that if you take them from my room and hide them, I'll tell your mother!'

'Oh, we won't hide them! said Snip. 'We'll call them from your room this very minute – and we'll send them rushing up the road as fast as can be – off to the Land of Rubbish, as sure as eggs are eggs!'

'I don't believe a word of it,' said Meddle, scornfully. 'If I *see* my stockings rushing by, I'll believe it, certainly – but not until. Magic like that isn't learnt by kids like you!'

A bicycle came down the lane. Tippy was riding it. Snip and Snap didn't smile at him, and he didn't wave to them. Meddle didn't know him.

'Just wait till this bicycle's gone by', said Snip. 'Ah, he's gone. Now then – STOCKINGS, COME BY AND RUN AWAY!'

Something black and wriggly now appeared a little way down the road. It was Meddle's stockings, tied to the distant bicycle with long black thread. The thread couldn't be seen – but here came the stockings, wriggling along fast like excited black snakes!

They passed in half a moment, and Meddle clutched at Snip and Snap in horror.

'Oooh! I say – they *did* look like my stockings! Snip, is it magic? Snap, don't do this. I don't like it. Were those really my stockings?'

'Of course,' said Snip, trying not to laugh. He saw the next bicycle coming, with Jinky in the saddle. He nudged Snap.

124

'And now I think we'll call for Meddle's footbal[l] boots to come!' said Snap. 'BOOTS, COME B[Y] AND RUN AWAY!'

Jinky had gone by on his bicycle, grinning, bu[t] not looking at Snip or Snap. Meddle looked dow[n] the road in alarm. What was this jigging along[?] Could it be – could it *really* be – his football boots[?]

'It is, it is! It's my boots!' cried poor Meddle[,] looking quite pale. 'Oh, stop, boots! Stop! Ther[e] they go, my lovely boots!'

And there they went, jigging along the road o[n] the black thread, Jinky's distant bicycle pulling them fast. They looked most peculiar.

'Snip! Snap! Don't do any more magic,' waile[d] Meddle. 'I don't like it. It's horrible. I've lost m[y] stockings and now my boots.'

Impy came by on his bicycle next, pedalling fast[,] afraid that he might explode into laughter at th[e] sight of Meddle's face. Snip called out, as soon a[s] he had gone by:

'FOOTBALL, COME BY AND RUN AWAY!'

'No, no!' begged Meddle. 'Not my football. No[t] my fine, splendid football! Oh, my, oh, my – it'[s] coming! It's coming, as sure as anything! And [I] daren't stop it, I daren't. I'm afraid I might go of[f] to the Land of Rubbish, too!'

Snip and Snap turned away to laugh. The foot[-]ball bounced along like a live thing, leaping high in the air if it touched a stone or a rut. It went b[y] at top speed, and Meddle sat down on the kerb an[d] groaned.

'Snip and Snap, I'll never meddle with your things again, never. Please, please, stop this. I'm frightened, I'm very . . . oh, my goodness me, is this something else coming?'

Heyho had cycled by, and behind him at a good distance came the cricket bat, sliding along fairly smoothly, but giving little jigs when it passed over a stone. Snip giggled. Meddle covered his face with his hands as soon as he heard Snap shouting to the bat to come by and run away.

'There goes my wonderful bat! Is there no end to this? Snip, forgive me. Now that I see my own treasures rushing off to the Land of Rubbish I know how you must have felt when I lost your ball and your watch and spoilt your stockings, and gave your pudding to the cat, and . . .'

'All right. We'll stop the magic now,' said Snip, with another giggle. 'We did think of sending your trunk off, too, but we thought we'd better not, or you might live with us the rest of your life if you'd no trunk to pack to go away.'

'I'm going away,' said Meddle. 'I'm leaving you tomorrow. You're too magic for me! I'd be afraid of ever borrowing anything again. And do you know what I'm going to do before I go?'

'No. What?' asked Snip and Snap.

'I'm going to get some money out of my bank,' said Meddle, 'and I'm going to buy a new watch and a new ball, and new stockings for you, and all the things I've ever borrowed and lost I'll buy and give you. This has been a lesson to me. My good-ness – how magic you are!'

Snip and Snap were surprised to hear all this. They looked at one another, feeling rather awk-ward.

'Well, if you really are sorry – and will really buy us all the things you've borrowed and spoilt and lost – maybe we'll use our magic to get back the things of yours that have rushed by this evening, and disappeared,' said Snip.

Meddle beamed. 'Will you really? That's grand of you! I'm afraid of going to the Land of Rubbish to fetch them.'

'Yes. They might keep you there,' said Snap, and giggled. 'All right, Meddle, it's a bargain – you buy us new things in place of the ones you've lost or spoilt and we'll get all your things back for you!'

Well, of course, it was easy to get them back, as you can imagine! They just went round to Tippy's the next day, and found Tippy, Jinky, Impy and Heyho there with all the things quite safe – and what a laugh they had together when they remembered how everything had rushed by the night before!

Meddle went out that morning, got some money and brought a whole lot of new things. He gave them to Snip and Snap and his Aunt Amanda. He packed his trunk. He sent a note to the station to

ask a porter to fetch it. He really seemed quite a different person!

He was very glad to have his stockings, boots, ball and bat back. He looked at Snip and Snap in awe and admiration.

'I never knew you were so magic,' he said. 'You frighten me! My word, I'm going to be careful in future!'

He said good-bye and off he went, swinging his stick in the air.

'I say,' said Snip, suddenly. 'Meddle lost his stick last week. Whose stick was that? It wasn't our VERY BEST ONE, was it?'

They rushed to the hall-stand to see if their stick was there. It was gone. Their mother called out to them.

'Meddle has borrowed it. He says he'll send it back next week.'

But will he? Snip and Snap can't make up their minds if he will or not – and neither can I! What a joke they played on Meddle, didn't they? I wish I'd been there to see it.

13: *You're a Nuisance, Mister Meddle!*

One day Mister Meddle took a little walk round the village. It was a lovely sunny day, and he had on his new suit and felt rather proud of himself.

'I hope everyone notices my new suit,' he thought. 'Ah, good morning, Mrs. Thump – *what* a lovely day! Oh, hallo, Mr. Woolly, I hope I see

you well! Ah, and here is dear Miss Scurry – how are you today?'

Nobody bothered to stop and talk to Meddle or to admire his new suit. He was very disappointed. He walked on and came to Mrs. Puff's dear little cottage. Roses grew all over it, and in her garden were fruit trees of many kinds. Ah – plums! Meddle saw them hanging purple and juicy on the trees.

He saw Mrs Puff at the front door, doing something to her roses. He decided to go and be polite to her – then she might offer him a basket of plums!

So in at the front gate he went. He took off his fine new hat and bowed. 'Good morning, Mrs. Puff. *What* a lovely day!'

'Oh – it's you, Meddle,' said Mrs. Puff, not sounding very pleased. 'How's your Aunt Jemima? Have you been annoying her lately? She told me what a trial you are at times, meddling and muddling.'

'That wasn't very nice of her,' said Meddle, offended. 'But she is often very difficult to please. *Very!*'

Mrs. Puff stood on her tiptoes to try and reach a rose-spray that had got loose. 'There now!' she said. 'I knew I wouldn't be able to reach it.'

'Pray let *me*,' said Meddle, at once. 'In fact if I can do anything for you, dear Mrs. Puff, I will – anything! I am always willing to help my aunt's friends.'

'I don't think I want your help, thank you, Meddle,' said Mrs. Puff, hastily. She knew too well

what a nuisance Mister Meddle could be when he tried to help. 'I'll get my husband to fetch the ladder and tie up that spray for me when he comes in. He's busy just now.'

She went into the house and shut the front door. 'Bother!' thought Meddle. 'She didn't offer me any plums – and I don't quite like to knock on the door and ask her for some. Well – I must be on my way, I suppose. What a pity she didn't notice my new suit!'

He was just walking down the path to the gate when he caught sight of a ladder in the garden. It was leaning against a plum tree, Mister Meddle stopped and looked at it.

Suppose he fetched it, put it against the front porch, and neatly tied up that rose-spray for Mrs. Puff – and a few others he could see were loose. Wouldn't she tell him to go and pick himself some nice plums for being so kind? Yes – surely she would!

Meddle went to fetch the ladder. It wasn't very heavy, so he put it over his shoulder and took it to the porch. He set it up and climbed it. He took some string from his pocket and began to tie up the rose spray, humming a little tune, and hoping that Mrs. Puff would hear it.

He tied up quite a lot of sprays, but Mrs. Puff didn't come out. Meddle was getting tired of standing on the ladder, tying up every spray within reach. He was tired of the roses, too – they had far too many thorns, and already he had torn his new suit in three places.

Then a loud voice shouted from somewhere. 'Hey! I want to get down! HEY!'

Meddle was surprised. Who wanted to get down? And why? He couldn't see anyone about.

The voice yelled again. 'I'm coming down! I've got enough now. HEY, I say – I want to get down!'

'Get down, then, whoever you are, and wherever you are!' shouted Meddle. 'Nobody's stopping you, are they?'

The front door opened and Mrs. Puff appeared. 'Meddle! Are you still here? Whatever are you doing to my roses – good gracious, you've tied the sprays so tightly that they look simply dreadful.

And where did you get that ladder?'

The loud voice yelled again from somewhere. 'HEY! Is that you, wife? I tell you, I want to get down. Did you take the ladder away? Well, bring it back!'

'Good gracious – that's Mr. Puff, up the big plum-tree,' said Mrs. Puff. 'Meddle – did you take his ladder away? How DARE you?'

'Er – well – *I* didn't know he was up the plum-tree,' said Meddle. 'I just took the ladder for the roses.'

'BRING BACK MY LADDER!' shouted Mr. Puff, and Meddle got down the ladder in such a hurry that he caught his foot in one of the rungs and fell to the ground – bump! He got up and dusted himself.

'Take the ladder to Mr. Puff,' said Mrs. Puff, crossly. 'Really, Meddle, why must you *always* meddle in things that don't concern you! Now I'll have to untie all those sprays!'

Meddle ran to the big plum-tree with the ladder. He set it up against the tree. 'Sorry, Mr. Puff!' he called. 'I just . . .'

'Oh – so it was *you*!' cried Mr. Puff, and an angry red face appeared through the leaves. 'I might have guessed!' And, dear me, he threw a handful of ripe plums at poor Meddle! They burst all over his beautiful new suit.

Meddle fled. Mr. Puff looked so very angry that he was quite sure he would get a whole lot more plums in half a second. He ran down the road and

turned the corner. He almost bumped into his
Aunt Jemima.

'Now, now – look where you are going!' she
said. 'My goodness me, Meddle! Look at your
clothes! Torn – and dusty – and stained with
purple juice. How *can* you walk about like that?
Why don't you go and buy yourself a really nice
new suit? I'm ashamed of you!'

And away she walked, with her nose in the air.
Poor Meddle – in trouble again! If only he didn't
meddle in other people's business he'd be a lot
better off, wouldn't he?

14: *Good-bye, Mister Meddle*

Mister Meddle always liked roaming round the railway station. It was a most exciting place, with trains puffing in and out, people hurrying all about, and porters shouting, 'Mind your backs, please!'

One morning he went into the station, and sat down on a seat to watch what was going on. He saw the people buying their tickets, carrying their luggage, looking for their trains.

'They all look very *worried*,' said Meddle to himself. 'Very worried indeed. Perhaps I'd better help some of them.'

Now, Meddle, as you know, was exactly like his name. If he *could* poke his long nose into anything and meddle with it, he was happy! So up he got to see what he could do.

He met a little man panting and puffing, carrying a very heavy bag. Meddle went up to him and tried to get hold of it. 'Let me help,' he said.

'Certainly not. Let go,' said the man, fiercely. 'I know what you'd do if I let you take my bag – run off with it! And that's the last I would see of it.'

'What a dreadful thing to say!' said Meddle, and stalked off crossly. He bumped into a woman who was carrying three parcels and dragging a little dog along too. 'Allow me, Madam!' said Meddle politely, and took the biggest parcel from the woman.

The dog immediately flew at him and nipped his leg. Meddle dropped the parcel and howled. There was a crash!

'There now!' said the woman, angrily. 'I had my best glass bowls packed in that parcel! What do you think you are doing, snatching it from me?'

'Your horrible dog bit me,' said Meddle, most annoyed.

'Well, of course he did!' said the woman. 'He thought you were stealing my parcel. It served you right. Please call a porter and ask him to clear up this mess of broken glass – and you will have to pay

me forty pence for breaking the bowls.'

A porter came up. '*I* saw you meddling!' he said to Meddle. 'If parcels want carrying, *I'll* carry them. It's my job, not yours. And *you* can clear up the mess, because that's your job, not mine!'

Well, you would have thought that Meddle would have had enough of poking his nose into other people's affairs by then, wouldn't you? Not a bit of it! He paid the angry woman forty pence, he cleared up the mess – and then he went around looking for somebody else to meddle with.

He saw a little man, a big, plump woman, and four children all trailing along. 'Oh dear, oh dear!' said the woman. 'We shall miss the train, I know!

Where do we get our tickets?'

'Madam, over there,' said Meddle, hurrying up to her. 'Shall I hold the children's hands while you get them?'

'No, thank you,' said the woman. 'They can hold each other's hands. Dad, get your money ready for the tickets. Oh dear, what a queue there is at the ticket-office!'

'Madam, you go and get your seats in the train, and I'll buy the tickets for you,' said Meddle.

'Do go away!' said the little man, crossly. 'I'm not leaving you here with my money, I wouldn't be so silly!'

'That's not a nice thing to say at all!' said Meddle, most offended. 'Do you mean to say I'd run off with the money? Well, I never heard such a —'

'Do please go away,' said the plump woman. 'We can look after ourselves all right. Oh my, oh my, what a queue. I wish these people in front of us would hurry up, I know we shall miss our train.'

'We'll catch it all right,' said the little man, looking at the station clock. 'But if it's crowded we shan't get any seats, that's certain.'

The children began to cry. 'I want a seat,' sobbed one. 'I want to look out of the window.'

'Shall I go and get some seats for you?' said Meddle, quite determined to help in some way. 'I could go and find a carriage and put newspapers and things on six seats — then no one would take those seats, and when you came along you could

have them. I could hop out of the carriage and wave good-bye.'

'What an extraordinary fellow!' said the little man to his wife. He turned to Meddle. 'I tell you, we don't want people poking their noses into our business.' he said. 'We can't stop you finding seats, of course, and spreading them with newspapers and coats to keep them for us! I can see you mean to interfere with us in *some* way!'

'Not interfere – just *help*,' said Meddle, quite hurt. 'All right – I'm off to get some seats for you. I'll buy some newspapers to spread on them, so that people will know they are reserved for others!'

He turned away, pleased. He bought some papers and then ran to find the train. Bother! He had forgotten to ask which one it was. It must be the very next train leaving, because the little man and his wife were in such a hurry to get the tickets. One of the children had said they were going to the sea – now which train would it be?

'Ah – here's one leaving in five minutes – to Seaside Town,' said Meddle. 'This must be it. How glad they will be when they come rushing on to the platform, find the train is full – but with six seats saved for them!'

He bought a platform ticket and hurried to the train. He found a carriage that was quite empty. Good! He sat down, and arranged four newspapers and his overcoat on five seats. He sat in the sixth himself, of course.

He felt pleased with himself. 'It's so nice to help

people,' he said. 'Now that little family will all travel comfortably to the seaside, each with a nice seat all the way.'

People looked into the carriage, saw the newspapers and coat on the seats and went on again. Meddle grinned. Aha! He had been very clever, he thought.

The minutes went by. Meddle began to feel anxious. Surely those people wouldn't miss the train? He looked out of the door. There was no sign of them. Oh dear – should he go and hurry them up?

Meddle got out some pennies to give to the children when they came. One fell from his hand and rolled under the seat. Oh dear! Meddle got down to get it. It was right in the far corner. Meddle had to get half-way under the seat to reach it.

A loud whistle blew. PHEEEEEEEE! Meddle jumped. He tried to wriggle out from under the seat, but somehow or other he got stuck. 'Wait, wait! Tell the engine not to go yet!' shouted Meddle, from under the seat. But nobody heard him, of course. The engine began to puff out smoke and then, with a rattle and rumble and clatter, the train began to pull out of the station!

Meddle wriggled himself free and rushed to the window. He leaned out, shouting loudly, trying to open the door. It was a good thing he couldn't, because the train was now going quite fast.

'Stop! Stop! Let me out!' yelled Meddle. 'I'm not going, I tell you!'

143

But he was. He couldn't help it! And the last thing that poor Meddle saw was the little man and his family all getting calmly into another train marked 'To Golden Sands' – and finding plenty of seats, too!

'This *wasn't* their train!' groaned poor Meddle. 'And *what* will the ticket-inspector say to me if he comes and finds me without a proper ticket and all the seats to myself? Oh dear – this is what comes of helping people.'

No, Meddle – that's what comes of meddling! There he goes, all the way to the sea, first stop Seaside Town!